BOUNCE

NATASHA FRIEND

SCHOLASTIC INC.
New York Toronto London Auckland Sydney
Mexico City New Delhi Hong Kong Buenos Aires

This book was originally published in hardcover by Scholastic Press in 2007.

ISBN-13: 978-0-439-85353-8
ISBN-10: 0-439-85353-2

12 11 10 9 8 7 6 5 4 3 2 1   9 10 11 12 13 14/0

Printed in the U.S.A.   40

First Scholastic paperback printing, April 2009

To my brother, Nick.
How can this not be for you?

CHAPTER ONE

Here is how Birdie drops the bomb:

He takes us to the best restaurant ever — Cook's, on Bailey's Island — and he says we can order whatever we want. This means a full lobster dinner for Mackey and a tuna roll for me, plus fries. He waits until our tongues are busy celebrating before he lets it fly.

"Kids, I'm getting married." Then, "We're moving to Boston."

And there you have it. Blammo!

Life as we know it, over.

Mackey keeps eating like nothing has happened, grabbing steamers by their slimy black necks and dunking them in butter. All he does all day is eat and play computer games. You would think he'd weigh five hundred pounds by now, but he doesn't; he's a beanpole. Six feet two skinny inches, and he's only fifteen. I know a lot of people call him Lurch behind his back, or Pizza Face because of his zits, and he is not exactly the most popular kid on the block, but I have to confess he is my brother. Who right now is my only ally.

"Ahem," I say, and kick Mackey under the table. But he just grunts and grabs a bunch of fries off my plate. So I stare across the table at our father. "How are you getting *married*? You *just met*."

"I know," Birdie says, smiling. "Isn't it remarkable?"

Remarkable.

Nauseating is more like it. Stomach-churning. Upchuckingly unbelievable is what it is.

Birdie asked Eleni Gartos to marry him and she said yes. After two months of dating, she said yes. To *Birdie*. Why?

Don't get me wrong. I love my dad. I do. But there are some indisputable facts here. First, the name: Albert. His friends call him Bert, and we call him Birdie — weird, I know, but we come from a proud line of hippies who call their elders whatever they want. Anyway, it's Albert. Then there's the beard with oyster cracker crumbs in it. And the big dork glasses and beak nose. If you really want to know, there are also a few black finger-nails from when his hammer slipped. And he wears overalls, which aren't what you would call fresh off the clothesline. Sometimes you want to take him by the shoulders and say, I know you're a carpenter, man, but come on! A little effort here, please!

But Birdie would just laugh. He doesn't care about looks or what people think. His theory is: Why shop at The Gap when you can get the same thing at Kmart for less? He is baffled that I want jeans with a certain label on them, not that we could afford them anyway. We are not exactly rolling in it. Which leads me back to my original question: Why would she want to marry him?!

"I can't believe this is happening," I say.

"I know," Birdie says. "I *know!*"

But he's missing the point, which is I can't believe he is doing this to us, his own children, who only left him alone for eight weeks.

I think back over the letters he sent me and Mackey at camp. Letters about our dog, Clam, and about how the tomatoes were growing. Letters with cutouts from the Sunday funnies. Jokey letters. Harmless letters.

Until a few weeks into it, when he started adding these stupid P.S.s at the bottom.

P.S. I'm working on a cottage in Kennebunkport. The renter's a college professor, from Boston. Very interesting woman. Great cook.

P.S. In case you were wondering (was anyone wondering?) her name is Eleni. Eleni Gartos. She has a Ph.D. in art history. Care to know the difference between Monet and Manet? Let me enlighten you!

P.S. Eleni doesn't have plans next weekend. I thought I'd bring her along for Visiting Day. Any objections?

And what did I say? Nothing. Absolutely zilch. I didn't even write back. It kills me that I didn't write back. It kills me that when she came for Visiting Day her presence barely registered. I was too concerned with where we would stash the candy Lindsay Meyer's parents brought, so our counselors wouldn't bust us.

"Ev?" Birdie is looking at me now. "You okay?"

I don't say anything.

There's a blob of clam chowder in his beard. Normally, I would point this out, and he would waggle his eyebrows and say he's saving it for later, and I would laugh.

But right now I don't feel like laughing.

I rack my brain, trying to remember what Eleni looks like. Whether she's divorced like Birdie's last girlfriend, LeeAnn, or a widow like Jill, the nurse he dated a few years back. Whether she has children. I vaguely remember Birdie mentioning a daughter.

"She has a girl, right?" I say. "My age?"

Birdie clears his throat, nods.

"Great," I say low. I stick my straw in the ketchup, smear it around on my plate, make a masterpiece.

A stepsister. Just what I need. My friend Ann has a stepsister, Brittany, and she's the devil. Now I too will have someone to steal my jeans and photocopy my diary.

Mackey grunts. "I thought it was a boy."

Birdie picks up his iced tea, takes a sip, sets it down again. "It is. I mean, you're both right. She has six kids. Four daughters and two sons."

Six kids.

Six.

Six kids that we will soon be related to.

It's too much even for Mackey. A mouthful of chowder flies out of his mouth and onto the table. "What is she," he says, "Irish?"

Birdie hands him a napkin. "Greek, actually."

I wait for Mackey to give him the business, say, *Well, we're not moving to Boston with a bunch of strangers. I don't care if they're Irish, Greek, or Siamese — you can just forget it!*

But Mackey doesn't say that. He says, "Can I get two desserts?"

Typical.

Fifteen-year-old brothers miss the point just the way fathers do. It's that apple-and-tree thing. They are the same kind of dense.

I am more of the feeler type, with my heart big and swollen in my throat. Our world has just been blown to smithereens. The Linney family, annihilated. How anyone could eat strawberry shortcake right now is beyond me.

CHAPTER TWO

When I was little, I spent all of my birthday wishes on the same thing: a mother. Also pennies in the fountain. And gray-headed dandelions. Stars. Turkey wishbones. Loose eyelashes. I would close my eyes tight, like the rules say, and whenever someone asked, *What did you wish for, Ev?* I would keep my mouth shut. Because if you tell, it won't come true.

The trouble with wishing is you get your hopes up every time. You really believe it will happen, and then, when it doesn't, you're depressed. Plus you have wasted your wish on a long shot when maybe if you had just asked for something reasonable like an A on the vocab quiz, the wish fairies would have said, *Okay, let's give her this one.*

One thing I've learned from my wishing over the years is how childish it is. Right up there with Santa Claus and training bras. If you're thirteen, you are too old for wishing. You are the age when you need to learn to make things happen for yourself.

Well, I am thirteen today. And my present to me is no more wishes. When Birdie puts that cake down on the table, I will do the blowing-out part, but that's all. It takes some pressure off, knowing I don't have to hit all the candles in one shot anymore. I can take as many breaths as I want.

It will be weird, though, not wishing. I have so many mother-daughter movies stored up in my head.

There's one with us in the kitchen, punching out bread dough side by side. She's wearing an apron — red with white checks — and has a smudge of flour on her cheek. I'm wearing a mini version of her outfit. There are flowers on the table — usually tulips, sometimes daffodils. When the timer dings, we take the bread out of the oven and slather it with butter and cinnamon sugar, and it's so good we'll eat the whole loaf.

Then there's us at the mall, walking into any store we want, not just the bargain basements. We are dressed to impress, both of us, in jean skirts and leather shoes. Pumps for her, loafer flats for me. Her hair is perfect, swept up in a red-gold twist on top of her head, and when she reaches over to zip me into some new dress, she smells so good you want to breathe her in deep. Lemons and lavender and vanilla wafers at the same time.

Sometimes I picture us on a blanket in the backyard. The sky is black and stars are everywhere, billions of them. "Hey, Ev," she says. "See the Big Dipper?" Oh yeah, I tell her. And there's the North Star. "Polaris," she tells me. And takes my hand.

One person who has never made it into my movies: Eleni Gartos, college professor and mother of six, saying, "Sure, Birdie, I'll marry you and be Evyn's new mom!"

The only mother I have ever imagined is Sarah Elizabeth Linney, whose picture hangs over the fireplace. She is very beautiful and warm-looking. She has long, straight hair and green eyes like a cat's. And with that she made my father fall in love in two seconds, at a party. Birdie was a goner.

The reason the fairy tale ended was a car crash. When I was one year old and Mackey was three, she was coming home from the drugstore and it was raining and she lost control of the wheel and hit a tree.

I don't remember her, not really. But she's in my head anyway.

Whenever I ask Birdie about my mom, he says the same thing: *She was too good for this world.*

Also in the top ten:

She was the most optimistic person you'll ever know.

Her smile could light up a room.

She didn't walk; she bounced.

I've heard it all, memorized every story — like the time she and Birdie went to McDonald's and she insisted on talking entirely in Mc's. *McHi. I'd McLike a McChicken McSandwich with McFries and a McCoke. . . . McHoney? McWhat would you McLike?*

She was always doing things like that, cracking Birdie up. You can tell, just by the photos, what a happy person she was. In every one, she's smiling. You look at that smile and you feel better. That's the kind of person she was. That's why she's the only mom I ever wished for — the only one I still want.

"You're going to love Eleni," Birdie says at dinner, passing around the chicken bucket. "She's great. And man, can she cook!"

"I *like* KFC," I say. I take a biscuit, slice it open, stuff in a pat of butter.

"Also," Birdie says, "she's brilliant."

I take a bite and say nothing.

"Ev. Just give her a chance, okay?"

"It's my birthday, Birdie," I say. "Could we not talk about this today? Please? For my birthday?"

Mackey stops shoveling food in his mouth for once and looks at me. "It's your birthday?" There's a corn kernel stuck to his lip, like a wart.

I break off a piece of biscuit, throw it across the table at him, peg his shoulder. "Yes, corn lip," I say. "It's my birthday."

Mackey shrugs and resumes steam shovel mode. Not even an ounce of guilt in his eyes. The food matters more.

"Thirteen," Birdie says, shaking his head. "I can't believe it."

"Me neither," I say.

There are so many things I can't believe right now. Too many to count.

At night, I talk to my mom. I know what people would say. *Talking to a dead woman? She must be nuts.* But I'm not.

Here's how to do it:

Turn off all the lights. Get comfortable in your bed. You should close your eyes, too; this is the best way to see her. Also, dress her in something comfortable, like a nightgown, hair loose, holding one of those tiny flip phones. That's what I do. Then, start talking. One tip: Don't expect her to always talk back. Sometimes she will and sometimes she won't. You just have to go with the flow.

I started talking to my mom when I was little. And I have always called her by a special name, Stella. Where I came up with that, who knows. Last year in Latin I learned that *stella* is another word for "star," which makes sense since I have always pictured my mom looking down on me from above, making sure I'm okay.

I know, I know. Heaven probably doesn't exist, and I'm probably a hypocrite because I never go to church except on Christmas, and that's only for the reindeer cookies. I don't know if God is real, but there is one thing I can tell you: When I talk, Stella listens.

Tonight our conversation is short.

Stell? It's me.

I think Birdie has a screw loose. That is the only explanation I can come up with for why he's doing this. WHY? Why is he getting married? Why do we have to move? Why did he give his thirteen-year-old daughter fluorescent-green leg warmers for her birthday? I don't even dance.

I'm looking for answers, but Stella doesn't have any for me tonight. She just smiles like always. She smiles and shakes her head as if to say, *That Birdie of ours. He's a funny one.*

CHAPTER THREE

Labor Day. While everyone else is on the beach, we're doing eighty down the Maine Turnpike. Everything we own is in a U-Move truck behind us, and 225 miles ahead, waiting, is our new life.

I begged Birdie, *begged* him to let me spend the first part of the school year in Maine. "What's the rush?" I said. "Can't we move in January? After Christmas, at least?" But noooooo. He wanted us to feel "settled" in our new "environment." Besides, rent was going up on our house, and did I have any idea how much heating oil would cost this winter? "You've got to be kidding me," I said. "You're getting married because of a little heating oil?"

And Birdie said no, no, of course not. That's when he sat me down and told me what a "great adventure" this was going to be for us. Full of "exciting new experiences." I was okay with it, right? Because if I wasn't, this was the time to tell him. Mackey and I were the most important people in his life. Our happiness was everything to him.

Well, what was I supposed to say?

I lean my head against the window and close my eyes.

Stell? It's me.

Buck up, is what she tells me. *Relax and enjoy the ride. Everything is going to be fine. Just fine.*

I want to believe her. I want to believe that my dead mother has the power to predict the future. But it's hard to stay positive when the car smells like dog — when Clam is in the crate at my feet, licking his crotch.

Mackey is in the seat beside me, headphones on, snoring. His zits are as bad as ever, and his hair is sticking up in front. Cowlick. He's wearing his *Star Trek* T-shirt with camouflage pants and brown hobbit sandals. When you look at him, here is what you think: Sci-fi Society, Chess Club, Band.

I reach over and grab his knee. "Hey," I say.

Mackey opens his eyes to slit level. "Huh," he says. "What?"

"You're snoring," I tell him. "It's bugging me."

I didn't mean to say that. I meant to say, "Mack, are you totally freaking out, too? Good! 'Cause I don't want to be the only one."

But I can't say it now because Birdie is in the front seat. You can tell he's in a great mood, too. He's whistling away, one of those hippie folk tunes he busts out for festive occasions. You can ask him nicely to stop, and he'll say okay, but then two seconds later he'll be at it again.

So I close my eyes and think about Jules. Jules Anthony, my best friend since diapers, whose backyard connects — *used to connect* — with ours. Jules, who taught me many important life skills, like how to flip my eyelids inside out, how to bake whoopee pies, how to stuff a bra. Jules, who took me aside at the fifth-grade class picnic to tell me that Mackey's old brown

12

plaid bell-bottoms were not my best look — who let me wear her favorite Bermudas instead.

Jules cried when I told her the news. Then she swore a bunch of times, which she does when she gets fired up. Me moving was a prime opportunity to try out some new swears I never heard before. Then it was my job to say something optimistic. *Hey, we'll still see each other. There's an Amtrak from Portland to Boston, don'tcha know. You can visit every weekend. Nothing has to change.*

But even I didn't believe myself.

"You can't leave, Ev," she told me the last time I saw her. "I won't let you."

"Jules —"

"No! You could stay here! Move in with us! We could adopt you!"

I flopped down on her canopy bed. She must have a thousand stuffed rabbits on that bed, even though she is thirteen and should know better. "I have to go," I told her. "Birdie's waiting."

"I know," she said. Then she swore a few more times and got teary. "I'm really gonna miss you."

I felt a lump in my throat the size of Texas. "Me, too."

On my way out the door, Jules said to wait. "We have to give each other something. You know, for friendship."

"Like what?" I said.

"Trade shirts."

"What? Now?"

"Seriously."

"Okay," I said.

And we did it, too. We stripped down to our bras right there on the Anthonys' porch in front of the entire neighborhood.

That is how I have on her cowgirl shirt right now, with the rhinestone buttons and frayed collar, and she has on the pink tie-dye I made at camp, halter style, so it showcases her belly button ring perfectly.

I am not really into the Western look, but I like that part of Jules is still with me. If I get sad, all I have to do is sniff the shirt and I am back on her canopy bed, surrounded by rabbits.

"This is it!" Birdie says.

He slows down and proceeds to wedge our station wagon into the tiniest spot you ever saw, approximately the size of a postage stamp. Then he jumps out to direct the U-Move guys where to unload.

I am sweating all over. My thighs are sticking to the seat like a couple of honey hams. I turn to Mackey and say, "This is a great adventure. Full of exciting new experiences."

He lets out a burp that smells like Egg McMuffin. Then he blows it in my face.

"You're disgusting," I say.

But now he is biting his nails down to bloody nubs, which tells me at least we're thinking the same thing. *Noooo!!! This cannot be happening! This sucks!*

When we get out of the car there she is, hugging Birdie. This is probably the tenth time I've seen them hug in the past two weeks, and it still makes me sick to my stomach. On Wednesday, when she drove up to Maine to help us pack, I caught them making out in the garage, and I almost threw up.

The way they're all over each other, you'd think he just got back from a war.

You can let go now. Seriously. You can let go of my dad. Any year now.

Finally, she does. She gives me and Mackey a big wave and starts walking over.

Here is the visual: head full of black curls, and short — even shorter than me. She barely comes up to Birdie's armpit, but she's curvy all over like the old Betty Boop cartoon he has framed in his shop. Therefore you understand right away what he sees in her. It is how all guys see: first, the body. Then, everything else.

"Hi, Evyn," she says, reaching out a hand for me to shake. Her nails are short and square. "Good to see you again."

I shake her hand, nod, try to smile. That is what Stella would do — smile at the woman we barely know, who is about to ruin everything.

"Mackey," she says to my brother, shaking his hand, too. "I'm so happy you're here."

He nods, then starts ripping his fingernails to shreds again.

"Okay," Eleni says, smiling. "Well . . . welcome!"

I stare at her teeth. There is lipstick on them, red.

One look at her and you do not think college professor. She has on black pants that are the low-rise variety. And high heels with the toes peeping through, red polish to match the lipstick.

Her T-shirt is plain white, the same kind Birdie wears, only on her it is tight in a womanly way, and there are no stains.

I have to admit she looks good for a mother — somebody else's. But not ours. Not now, not ever.

I know. She hasn't tried to hug us yet. Smart woman. She's playing it safe. But wait until they're married, and she starts planting cheek kisses left and right. I give her three weeks before she says, *You can call me Mom now, honey. And while you're at it, scrub the toilet bowl.*

That's what happened to Tamara Schacter, this girl I know. The minute her dad got remarried, Kiki the Stepmonster took over her entire life and destroyed it.

If anything like that happens here, I will run away, which would make Jules very happy, I can tell you. I would go back to Maine and live with her. I have no clue how I'd get there, since I have exactly three dollars to my name. But I'd find a way, that much I promise you. I would definitely find a way.

CHAPTER FOUR

I have to share a room with two Gartos girls who are twins that I will never be able to tell apart — not that it matters because they haven't exactly started talking to me yet. Their names are Clio and Cassandra, they are fifteen, and they are dark and curvy like their mom. Their hair is long, model-worthy, with center parts and no bangs.

I sit in the middle of the room on a cardboard box labeled EVYN CLOTHES, waiting for instructions. Finally, one of the twins turns to me and says, "That's your bed, over there." She points. "Storage drawers underneath."

"Oh," I say. "Okay. Thanks." Then, "You have a nice room."

The other twin rolls her eyes and snorts. "Cassi has a *thing* for incense," she says. "Just to warn you."

I nod.

The first one says, "Shut up, Clio!" Then she turns to me. "Clio has a *thing* about not shaving any part of her body. She's practically a gorilla."

"Oh," I say. "Well."

I go to my bed by the window and stare out at the back-yard, which is not a yard at all. It's a microscopic stone patio, with a few potted plants and lawn chairs scattered around. Birdie told us we were moving to the city, and things would look different. Uh-huh. At home, our backyard was two acres with trees to climb, a gazebo Birdie built himself, a frog pond, and a vegetable garden. Clam had room to roam. This yard is a joke.

And the house, that's another thing. It is four stories but it's attached on either side to other people's houses so there's no side yard and no driveway. Birdie calls it a brownstone — don't ask me why, since it is red brick.

Our old house had natural wood shingles and a porch swing. And out by the blueberry bushes, a birdhouse made to look exactly like ours. Picture a tiny wooden swing just for birds. That's the kind of detail you miss, once you are gone. You miss your birds' old porch swing.

"Where's my red sweater?" one of the twins is saying now. "Did you take my red sweater?"

And the other one says, all sassy, "What red sweater?"

And the first one says, "The V-neck! You better not have taken it, Clio, I swear to God. . . ."

Sometimes the feeling of missing a place is so big it makes you want to open your window and scream. But obviously I can't do this because the window isn't really mine. Neither is the bed I'm sitting on. Or the air.

Birdie comes to the door with a glass of water in his hand. His face is a million sweat beads to match his grungy shirt. But that doesn't stop me from jumping up and hugging him.

"Birdie," I say.

He squeezes me, kisses the top of my head. He smells like sweat and sawdust. I can feel his beard scruffing against my scalp. "Birdie," I say again.

"Ev," he says, pulling back and smiling. "Settling in?"

I look at him. His face says, *I've never been happier.* I grab his glass and take a sip. Then another.

"How goes it, girls?" Birdie says, turning to the sweater sisters, away from me. "Everything okay?"

One of the twins runs over and throws her arms around Birdie's neck. "Al!"

Al, whoever he is, ruffles her hair. "Clio!" he says.

The other one jumps all over him. "Don't let her touch you, Al! She's a criminal! She'll steal the shirt off your back!"

"Whoaaa," Birdie says, pulling away. "A criminal? In my very own home?"

All three of them laugh, and you can see the triangle of love blooming right there in the room. In Al's very own home.

"Hey, *Al*," I say later. "What's up, *Al*?"

And he says, "I'm still the same old Birdie."

Meanwhile his new family is downstairs, chopping onions and firing up the grill in Al's Diner.

I'm sitting on the edge of the bathtub, while Birdie brushes his teeth in the peach-colored sink. He is constantly brushing — and flossing, and picking, and fluoride rinsing. This is what happens when you have dentists for parents, like Birdie did. He knows way too much about gingivitis. On Halloween, the only thing he will hand out is apples: nature's toothbrush.

"Birdie," I say.

"Yeah," he says, then spits in the sink.

"I don't know if I can live here."

Birdie turns to me. "This is a big transition, Ev. It's going to take some time to get used to."

"Uh-huh."

"Are you willing to give it some time?"

I don't know if I'm willing or not, but one thing I do know is I hate this peachy bathroom — and everything in it.

"Question," I say. "Why are all the toiletries freakishly large?"

Birdie holds up a ten-gallon bottle of mouthwash and grins.

"Seriously," I say. "What's up with that?"

Birdie unscrews the top and pours himself a cup. He says that a family as big as this one needs to shop in bulk. "B.J.'s," he says. "I'll take you sometime."

Everything there is econo-sized, he tells me. You can even buy clothes.

I picture myself on the first day of school, econo-sized, like Paul Bunyan. XXXXXXL plaid shirt, clown boots, pencil the size of a telephone pole.

"Birdie?" I say.

"Yeah." He is flossing now.

"How much time?"

"Huh?"

"How much time do I have to give it?" I say. "A week? Two weeks? A month? What?"

Finally, he walks over to me.

"What if this was a big mistake?" I say. "What then?"

Birdie puts his hands on my shoulders. "And what if it wasn't?" he says. "I'm just playing devil's advocate here, but what if this was the best thing that ever happened to us? Can you at least leave yourself open to the possibility that this could be great?"

I make my head nod. *Sure, Al. Well, gotta go throw myself under a train now.*

It's dinner, and I am sitting between the oldest Gartos girl, Thalia, and the youngest, Phoebe. Mackey is flanked by the sweater twins, who are still squabbling. Not that he minds. He is like one of those cartoon cats, eyes popping out of his head every time he looks at one of them. *Boooiiinnnggg!*

Guys don't look at me like that. Ever. But I'm used to it.

One time when Jules and I went to the mall, a bunch of jocks in letter jackets wolf whistled as we walked by — at both of us, I thought. They came over, but only to talk to Jules. I noticed they never looked directly at her face but at her white tank top, where all the action was.

"Guys love you," I said later, but Jules just laughed and said, "Guys love anything with mammaries."

Right now the only person at the table with mammaries smaller than mine is Phoebe, and she's six. The first thing she said when I sat down was, "Are you a boy?" and I said, "It's Evyn with a *Y*, not Evan with an *A*" — my stock answer, which doesn't explain such problems as my hair (chop cut), my outfit (Mackey's old sweats), or my chest (non-existent).

"I have three sisters," she tells me. "And two brothers."

"Yes," I say. "I know."

The brothers are sitting across from me at this moment. The younger one, Ajax (if you can believe that anyone would name their son after a cleanser), is my age. He is shaped like a brick, and all he talks about so far is sports. Apparently, he is the star forward on the eighth-grade soccer team, and we are all supposed to watch him play in a scrimmage on Saturday. Goody.

The older one is a different story. Ever since he sat down I haven't been able to stop sneaking glances at him. His name is Linus, and I know what you're thinking, but you are wrong. This Linus is no thumb-sucker. He's nineteen years old, first off, with stubble on his chin. Also he is tall, with big shoulders, brown eyes like M&M's, and dark curls flopping on his fore-head. I think about those curls all through dinner — how it might feel to grab hold of one of them and pull, then watch it spring back into place.

I have to pinch myself. *No drooling at the table.*

Linus eats everything Eleni puts on his plate: olives, stuffed grape leaves, stinky cheese. He has lamb juice on his chin when he says, "Why can't you cook in my dining hall?"

Eleni pats his arm and says, "Move home."

It kills me that he lives in a dorm, not with us.

Linus laughs. "How can I move home? All the beds are taken."

You can have my bed, I think. *I'll sleep in the storage drawers.*

Then I open my mouth. "So. Linus. What's your major?" This is the question grown-ups are always asking Jules's sister, Agnes, whenever she comes home from Yale.

Linus looks at me for the first time, and his face says, *Who are you?*

I look down at my plate, which has suddenly become fascinating; it's not just a pile of lamb, it is a landscape of pink. Not unlike my face.

"I'm thinking about poli-sci," Linus says. "Maybe econ. I don't know."

He tells us he isn't sure what he wants to do when he graduates. "I don't really see myself in politics," he says. "Or crunching numbers all day. I'll probably move to Vail and be a professional ski bum."

I went skiing once. With Jules, when her dad got free passes. My first time down the mountain I thought I was doing great — taking my time, making nice wide turns — when some guy in gold snowpants whizzed past me, yelling, "This isn't the giant slalom trail, moron!" When I tried to flip him the bird, I wiped out and broke my arm.

Professional ski bum. Huh.

I picture Linus at the top of a snowy peak, holding a cup of change and one of those homemade signs. WILL SLALOM FOR FOOD.

Birdie says, "There are worse things to do with a college degree."

"True," I say.

Now everyone is looking at me, so I am forced to continue. "You could be a pirate."

Linus smiles when I say this. His teeth are as white as a box of Chiclets — a dentist's dream. Linus has dream teeth. When he says to me, "Very funny," my stomach jumps up and does the mambo.

CHAPTER FIVE

In the morning, I go up to the attic and stand around in my underwear. This is because I'm getting measured for the ugliest bridesmaid's dress in history. Thalia, the eighteen-year-old, is in charge. She says there's only one way to ensure a perfect fit. "Don't move," she tells me. And I obey. Thalia has a way of making people listen. There are a lot of sharp pins in her mouth, for one thing. And she has a voice like a principal. You don't want to end up in her office after school.

There are also many things a guy would fall in love with. Hair: a brown velvet curtain. Eyes: two black pools. Tan skin. She's wearing a camisole with a flowy skirt and bare feet, and she walks like a ballerina — toes turned out.

"Don't move," she says again, through her mouthful of pins. "I might stick you."

I see that her eyebrows meet in the middle.

"I'm not," I say.

She winds a strip of cloth around my torso and yanks it tight.

Oh, this dress is going to be so hideous. First, it's orange. It is the kind of orange that makes you want to say, "Hey! Is there a pumpkin festival this afternoon? Great!" Plus, it's toga style. I know all about this from Latin class, where we learned how to make togas for extra credit. They are not flattering, even if mine did win second prize.

"This cut is fantastic on you," Thalia tells me, before I can run out of the room. She pulls the cloth tighter. "You have a great little figure."

I look down at my flat chest, even flatter now, and sigh.

"Almost done," she says, jabbing me in the ribs with a pin.

"Ow!"

"Oh! Did I stick you?"

I look at her face to see if she's sorry.

"I can't believe my mother is making me do this," she says. "I take one sewing class, and she thinks I'm an expert." Her eyebrow is furrowed. "Sorry."

"That's okay," I tell her.

"Well, you know what they say. *Beauty is pain.*" Thalia turns me by the shoulders to the full-length mirror. "Ta daaaa!"

We both stare at me.

Then Thalia adds a wreath of flowers to my head — orange and yellow and brown all strung together. "Gorgeous," she says, and for a minute I actually feel it. I am the queen of the pumpkin parade. I am riding atop a leaf-covered float, waving daintily to the crowd. Tossing candy corn in the air like confetti.

Maybe at the wedding, Linus will take one look at me and think, *Shazam!* At the reception, he will walk over, all shy and handsome in his tux, curls bouncing on his forehead. *Good evening, Evyn*, he will say. Then, *May I have this dance?*

Thalia squeezes my arm. "You and Phoebe are going to be adorable."

"Adorable," I repeat. Huh.

"Have you seen the flower girl baskets?" Thalia smiles, and I see that her front teeth overlap. "You'll love them," she says, meaning it.

I open my mouth but nothing comes out.

Flower girl baskets.

Flower. Girl. Baskets.

I am not a bridesmaid. I am a flower girl.

"I'm thirteen," I say.

Thalia raises her eyebrow.

"Never mind," I mumble.

"Thirteen is tough," she tells me. She takes the wreath off my head and begins packing it in tissue. "I remember thirteen."

"Right," I say. I use my most sarcastic voice because I'm thinking, *You don't remember squat.*

When I tell Mackey, he says, "Mmph."

This is how he responds in our conversations, like a caveman. Also, he never looks at me. He's always staring at a computer screen, or at one of those books with dragons and amulets on the cover, and titles you can't pronounce.

Today it's *The Sword of Arzaksband,* which he is reading from the top bunk, while his new roommate, Cleanser Boy, is at soccer practice.

I am sitting in a galaxy far, far away from the bottom bunk. Because — I can tell just by looking — it smells like socks.

"I'm thirteen," I say. "Thir*teen,* Mack."

Mackey flips a page, says, "Hrmp."

He obviously doesn't care, but I keep going — because it feels good to let it out. I say, "These people are idiots." Then I feel bad. "I mean, don't they know I'm too old to be a flower girl?"

Mackey stops reading and tries some English. "I have to wear a tux," he says.

I say, "Togas and penguin suits don't go together."

He shrugs, starts to read again — his way of telling me the conversation is over.

"So," I say. "What are we going to do about this?"

Silence.

"*Mack*," I say.

"Hunh."

"I think Birdie's judgment is seriously impaired."

Finally, Mackey closes his book and looks at me. "Maybe he's sick of being alone. Don't you want him to have someone?"

"He has us," I say.

"It's not the same thing."

I stare at the giant zits on Mackey's nose. They're red and pussy — gross. He washes his face and uses that Clear-Skin stuff every night, but nothing works. Who does Mackey have to hang out with? The Lord of the Rings. Spock. He doesn't have a Jules. The only person he ever brought home was Willy Grimes, who wore high-waters and ended up stealing most of Mackey's action figures.

Sometimes I look at my brother and think, *Ouch.*

"Well," I say now. "Let's just hope Birdie knows what he's doing."

Mackey grunts. His eyes are on the book.

"Okay." I walk backward, toward the door. "I guess I'll be going, then. Off to put on some Underoos and play with my Hello Kitty dolls. You know. Thirteen-year-old stuff."

"Gngh," Mackey says. Which I guess means good-bye on his planet.

I have never tried talking to my mother from a bathroom before, lying fully clothed in a peach-colored tub, in the middle of the day. But there's a first time for everything.

Stella? It's me, Evyn. The oldest living flower girl. Did you see the dress? Barforama.

Stella smiles. *It's not so bad.*

Yes it is. Probably they will put me at the kids' table, too, with butter shaped like Mickey Mouse ears. And later, we will do the hokey pokey. I wish you were here to talk to Birdie for me, because I bet he would listen to you. "Honey," you could say. "Evyn's a teenager now. Let's not humiliate her at the wedding." But I guess if you were here, he wouldn't be getting married, would he?

Stella laughs. *I hope not!*

I wish you were here.

Oh, honey, she says. *Me, too.*

CHAPTER SIX

It's the first day of school. I am wearing an econo-sized back-pack, underwear that itches, and a lampshade.

Everyone else on the bus is wearing a lampshade, too, but that doesn't make me feel better. First, I am not a kilt person, and even if I were, I would not choose green-and-yellow plaid that bells out at the knees. However, at the March School for Girls, you don't get a choice.

"The dreaded lampshade," one of the twins said to me this morning, shuddering. "I wore that thing for eight years." She had on jeans, a silver spangle top, and beat-up cowboy boots.

And the other one said, "Oh, God. The lampshade." She said this from the comfort of her suede pants, plum-colored sweater, and giant hoop earrings. "You'll want to burn that thing in a week."

I just nodded. There was nothing to say except, *Where do you keep the lighter fluid?*

At breakfast, only two people looked as bad as me: Ajax, in a green-and-yellow-plaid blazer with *Thorne School for Boys* emblazoned on the pocket, and Phoebe, wearing a mini version of my outfit.

"I'm in the lower-school building," she told me. "It's yellow. You're in the middle-school building. It's green."

"Oh," I said. "Uh-huh."

Eleni plopped some scrambled eggs on the table and told me, "You're going to love the March School." Then, "That kilt looks darling on you."

Darling.

She had our lunches lined up in a row on the counter: seven brown bags with our names on them, folded down at the top.

After breakfast, I got Birdie alone. "This is not good," I told him. "Not good at all."

Birdie just hugged me and said the important thing was not the uniform but the quality of my education.

"It's not just the uniform," I told him. "It's everything."

"The March School is very reputable," he said. "Eleni tells me it was ranked third in the city for —"

I interrupted him. "I think I'm going to puke."

Birdie hugged me again, scruffing his chin along my scalp. "Be sure you brush your teeth afterward," he said. "Stomach acid dissolves tooth enamel."

I don't know if he was kidding or serious, but right now I really am nauseous. Every time the bus goes over a bump I can feel eggs rising in my throat.

I am the only person sitting alone. It's killing me, but I'm not about to ask Phoebe and her little friend Hannah if I can triple with them.

I wish Jules was here. Or even my brother, who at this moment is riding in a car with Thalia and the sweater twins, on his way to the public high school. When I said good-bye this morning, he was pale with red eyes.

"Are you okay?" I asked.

And he said, "Ungh."

It's Mackey's first day of school, too, and I keep forgetting how bad it is for him, being zitty and geek-smart and not remotely cool. He will probably walk into the cafeteria later and not know where to go. Because no one will wave him over.

Whereas I'm sure that at some point today, at least one person will come up to me and say, "Hey, are you the new girl?"

She may not be Miss Popular, but that's okay. In my old school, I was somewhere in the middle. Maybe she'll have braces, like Jules, or a funny accent, like my friend Raquel, or her nose will be a little squooshed, like Ann's. But she will be nice, holding out her hand and saying, "I'm So-and-so. Who are you?"

And I will tell her, and then she will ask me to sit with her at lunch.

That's one thing I can be glad of right now. At least I am not my brother.

When the bus stops and everyone gets up, I realize I'm dressed wrong. For one thing, I don't have long hair. I don't have long hair smoothed back in a velvet headband or pulled up in a high, shiny ponytail. Also, I'm not wearing knee socks, folded over just so. Or big black shoes with chunky heels. I have on plain white sneakers and Ped socks — the kind with the pom-pom at the ankle.

Right this second, Jules, Raquel, and Ann have on plain white sneakers and Peds with pom-poms, as they walk into my old school together, without me.

Now the bus driver is staring at me in the giant rearview mirror. "Sometime this month?"

I stand up and take off my Peds and stuff them into my backpack. Like this will be enough.

In homeroom, I'm seated between two girls who are wearing the correct hair-and-sock combo. They lean over and talk to each other like I'm not here.

"Did you watch *The E.B.* last night?" the one with the ponytail asks.

And the one with the headband says, "Natch."

I know what they're talking about, this TV show Jules and I used to rag on — where the kids act like adults and the adults act like kids, and everyone is tan, even in winter.

"Isn't Wyatt James sooooo petute?"

"Sooooo petute."

"I can't believe Brandi dumped him for Vincent."

"I know!"

"Brandi is a pita, anyway," Ponytail says.

"A *total* pita," says Headband. And they both laugh.

I sit absolutely still. I think about the only pita I know of, which is bread. I think about how Jules and I used to talk in code, too. She was "J-Dog." I was "E-Pup." A cute boy was a "Benny," and we were "Efftees" — Friends 'Til the End. Jules and I spoke the same language, so we understood each other.

Here, I understand every fifth word.

My first class is Latin, and the room is a closet. Literally. There are mops in here.

The Latin teacher, who is bald with furry arms, looks around for a window to open, but there isn't one. There's no chalkboard, either. And there's just one desk. For me. The only person in the school stupid enough to pick a dead language over Spanish.

I can't open my locker.

It's a combination lock. Three numbers — 5, 10, 15. Simple, right? But still I can't open it.

At my old school we had key locks. You carried your key on a cord around your neck, so there was never any problem.

I look around the hall for someone to help me, but there's no one here. The bell already rang. Which means I am late for math.

* * *

It's lunch, and I am standing in the middle of the cafeteria, holding a brown bag with my name on it, looking for someone to sit next to. Anyone.

There are clumps of girls everywhere — talking, laughing, eating. Probably they have all been friends since kindergarten, when they first ate paste together.

I bend down and pretend to tie my shoe. When I stand, someone is waving me over. Finally! She has messy hair, a long face, and big teeth. She looks like a horse. I could be friends with this girl.

I smile and start walking.

"Deebo!" she squeals. "I saved you a seat!"

Deebo?

A girl with a lunch tray breezes past me from behind. "Beebo!" She takes the seat next to Horse Face. They start giggling for no reason.

I am left in the dust, still holding a brown bag with my name on it. I would feel like a major loser right now, if anyone was looking at me. But nobody is.

I am Invisi-girl.

Stella? It's me, Evyn. I don't know why they call it study hall. It's not like anyone studies around here. See that group of headbands by the windows? They're text messaging, and cell phones aren't even allowed in school. I can't believe Birdie is making me go here.

Stella smiles.

I can't believe it's only sixth period. Two hours and 181 days until eighth grade is over. There's no way I'm going to make it.

Think positive, she says. Everything will work out fine. You'll see.

When I open the door, the house is silent. Apparently, I'm the only kid in Boston who had nowhere to go after school today. Phoebe has Brownies. Cleanser Boy has soccer. The sweater twins have student council. Even Mackey is going to watch Thalia try out for some dorky play.

I have nothing. I think I will go drown my sorrows in an econo-sized bag of Doritos. But when I get to the kitchen, there she is. The future Mrs. Birdie.

"Evyn!" she says, like she's been waiting for me all her life. "Come on in! I was just slicing up some baklava."

She smiles and wipes her hands on a towel. "How was your first day?"

I shrug. What am I going to say? *Super! The bus driver is my new best friend!*

"You must be hungry," she says, holding out a plate to me. "Have some. It's still warm."

She's right. I'm starving. It's hard to eat lunch when you're crouched in a bathroom stall for the entire period. But I don't tell her this. I tell her no, thank you. I say, "I think I'll go upstairs and start my homework."

She smiles wider. "Good for you. I wish everyone in this house were that motivated."

I'm halfway across the room when she says, "Evyn?"

I turn. "Yeah?"

"If you ever want to . . . you know, have anyone over after school or anything . . . well, I just want you to know that your friends are always welcome here. Anytime. You don't even have to ask. This is your home now, honey."

I nod, like I believe her.

She smiles, yet again.

Birdie is in my room, squatting on the floor, sawdust in his hair.

"Where were you?" I say.

He gets up. "Hrrrf?" There are three screws poking out of his mouth and a drill in his hand.

"When I got home from school. You're supposed to be waiting for me. You're always waiting for me when I get home from school. You. Not Eleni."

Birdie spits the screws into his hand. "I was up here. Building lofts." He gestures to a wooden structure in the middle of the room. "Cool, huh? It was Clio's idea. She thought if I built two —"

"Birdie."

"Yeah."

"Why is she even *home*? I thought she worked."

He puts down the drill and picks up a tape measure. "Her classes end at noon on Mondays. Mondays, she bakes."

"Uh-huh," I say. "She tried to make me eat baklava."

Birdie's eyes light up. "She made baklava? I love baklava."

"Birdie."

"What? You have something against baklava?"

"No. It's just —"

"You *have* to try it. Eleni makes incredible bakla —"

"Birdie!"

"What?"

"Stop saying *baklava*! You're missing the point!"

He raises his eyebrows at me. "Ouch. I used to have eardrums. What is the point?"

"Forget it."

"Ev. What is it?"

"Nothing. It's just . . . she's trying too hard. Okay? To be my buddy."

Birdie nods.

"I know you two are getting married, but she needs to just calm down. Enough with the smiling."

Again, Birdie nods. He strolls over to a stack of wood planks and grabs one. Then another.

"You know?" I say.

"Mmmhmm."

He snaps open the tape measure with one hand, starts measuring. "Lousy first day of school?"

"*What*? No! It has nothing to do with —"

Birdie looks up. "No?"

His eyes are warm and crinkly. I know I could tell him the

truth, if I wanted to. But right now I don't. I shake my head instead.

"Okay." He shrugs. "Jules called."

"She did?" This is the best news I've heard all day.

"Yep."

"When? I mean, when can I call her back? When do the rates go down?"

My father is an absolute maniac about the phone bill. We are only allowed to make calls at certain times, and then only if we dial this ridiculously long series of numbers first, so we can save two cents.

"Don't worry about that," he says now. "Just call."

"Are you serious?"

"Yep."

"Do I have to check with Eleni?"

"Nope."

"If you say so." I start for the door. Then I turn back. "Are we rich now or something?"

Birdie reaches into his beard and pulls something out — a wood chip maybe. "I wouldn't say *rich.*" He tosses it into the trash. "Comfortable."

"Comfortable," I repeat. "Huh."

"Define *comfortable,*" Jules says. "Because my uncle's a professor, and I can tell you they don't make diddly-squat. So the ex must be loaded. What does he do? Investment banker? CEO? Record producer?"

"I have no idea," I say. "Nobody tells me anything around here."

"Right," Jules says. And she knows to change the subject.

She launches into the first day of school and how awesome everything was. They repainted the eighth-grade corridor. Purple. It looks awesome. There's a new gym teacher, Mr. Dyer, who's awesome. All the girls are crushing on him, and guess who got him for an advisor?

On and on she goes until she finally remembers I'm on the other end. "So," she says. "How was school for you?"

I don't even miss a beat. "Awesome," I say. "Boston rocks."

CHAPTER SEVEN

On Saturday we go to Cleanser Boy's soccer game. I didn't want to come, but Birdie insisted. He mentioned such things as Family Unity and Show of Sibling Support. Also, Lunch.

"Eleni made us a picnic," Birdie said this morning. "Quesadillas. And brownies!"

I am beginning to think he's getting married just for the food.

At Casa Gartos, Birdie is becoming the world's leading expert on fine cuisine. He always seems to have something in his mouth, and it always seems to be the most delicious thing ever, because Eleni Made It.

Have you tasted this pesto? It's unbelievable. Eleni made it. Try this spanakopita. Eleni made it. It's out of this world!

In our old life, I was the one who cooked. Chicken potpie and manicotti. Pigs in blankets. Hash. Also, I sewed buttons on Birdie's shirts. And gave him foot rubs. I cut his hair, and I did as good a job as any barber.

Now, Eleni is the boss.

"Al," she said last night. "I'd really love you to be clean-shaven for the wedding."

Two seconds later, Birdie was beardless.

In my whole life I have never seen Birdie without a beard.

Even in pictures from when my mom was alive, there it was —
as much a part of him as his nose. Without it, he looks weird,
just vaguely familiar, like someone I've met before and can't
quite place.

Also, he's wearing new clothes. Khakis. A shirt that requires
ironing. Some stupid, preppy-looking jacket with a corduroy
collar. Birdie wouldn't be caught dead in that jacket. But *Al* is
the ultimate prepster.

Al eats pesto.

Al shaves.

And now, Al is climbing the bleachers to shake hands with
a bunch of Eleni's friends.

"Frank," she says, smiling like crazy. "This is Al Linney,
my fiancé. . . . Walter, Marlene. My fiancé, Al. . . . Jane? Gus!
Yoo-hoo! This is Al!"

The bleachers are full of Eleni's people.

Also full of my March School classmates, sans lampshades.
Today it's all about jeans and thigh-high boots.

"Do those girls go to March?" one of the twins asks me.
"Are they in your class? Are they cool?"

And the other one says, "Are you friends with them?
What are their names? I think the one with the blond hair is
Corey Ritterman's little sister. Do you know her? Is she a
Ritterman?"

"That's not Corey's sister. She looks nothing like her."

"Yes, she does."

"No, she doesn't. The hair, maybe, but that's it. Look at her
face. Her face is totally different."

"Want to bet? How much do you want to bet that girl is

a Ritterman? . . . Hey, do you know her? Her last name's Ritterman, right?"

I make myself smile and shrug. "I don't know," I say. "I'm still trying to put names with faces."

It's not exactly a lie. I just happened to leave out the fact that not one of those girls has talked to me yet. And that I have spent five consecutive lunch periods in the bathroom stall.

The sweater twins have a million friends. They are constantly at someone's house, or instant messaging, or on the phone. I'm pretty sure they wouldn't understand my predicament.

Right now a trio of high-school girls is climbing the bleachers. Clio and Cassi squeal and run over to them, and I'm left with Mackey, who has his headphones on full blast, and Thalia, who's knitting a woolly blue sausage.

"It's a garter," she explains. "*Something blue.* For my mom to wear under her dress."

"Oh," I say. "Uh-huh."

"She's all set for the old, new, and borrowed, so . . ."

"Ah," I say. "Good."

I look over at Eleni, who's got her hand on Birdie's thigh. It makes me mad, that hand, but I don't know why. I just want her to take it off. I try my mental telepathy trick, but that doesn't work. So I have to look away.

I turn my attention to the soccer field. The Thorne boys are all huddled together, chanting something I can't understand. A bullhorn blasts, somebody kicks a ball, and everyone in the bleachers starts cheering.

I don't get it. The game just started. Nothing's happened yet. Why all the excitement before we've even scored?

"Go, Gartoooos!"

I look around for the loudmouth and spot him, over by the fence. He is wearing a leather jacket and jeans with a tear in the knee.

He is tall with big shoulders.

And curls.

Curls flopping on his forehead in the most beautiful manner.

At one point he looks up and waves to us, and something comes over me. A warmth in my stomach. A buzzing in my ears and, I have to say it, a rapid heartbeat.

I know exactly what this is because I felt it all summer long. Whenever Darren Peet, the water-ski counselor, took off his sunglasses, I would get like this. Then, if he ever smiled at me, my face would turn bright red.

Jules calls it my crush-blush.

But Darren Peet was one thing. All the girls in my bunk loved him, the whole camp loved him, you were *supposed* to love him.

This is different. This is Linus, my nineteen-year-old almost-stepbrother. I'm pretty sure what I'm feeling is illegal.

The soccer game is a blur. I keep one eye on the field, pretending to be watching, while the other eye is stuck on the fence.

I'll say one thing, Linus knows his soccer. You can tell by the way he yells instructions. He understands exactly where

Ajax needs to go (*Deep! Deeeeep!*) and what he needs to do (*Shoot! Shooot!*).

At some point, when Ajax has the ball and is running up the field, Linus starts jumping around, clutching his head in his hands and bellowing — part orangutan, part mental patient.

Now I feel free to turn my head and stare with both eyes. Linus is way more interesting than soccer. There's something about him. It's not just his curls. Or his shoulders. Or his teeth. It's beyond looks. It's the entire package. It's his whole earsplitting, spastic person, and I am starting to understand the difference between a crush and real love. Darren Peet was nothing. Linus is —

Bam!

My head snaps back hard.

Oww.

Soccer ball.

Owwww.

Soccer ball. In the face.

Owwwwwwww, my nose.

"You're supposed to tip her head forward and pinch the bridge. Like this. Direct pressure."

Owwww.

"No. You have to tip her head *back* and put ice on her neck. That slows the bleeding."

"Are you insane? She'll choke."

"Shut up, Clio. I took first aid."

"*You* shut up, we took the same class. And I know for a fact —"

"Mom. Here. It's all I could find."

Owwwww.

"Evyn? Sweetheart? Fresh tissues. Here, let me take those. . . . Your dad's getting some ice. There you go, keep the pressure on. That's it."

"See? I *told* you, Cassi."

"Thalia, honey, go see what's taking Al so long. . . ."

"Hey. Tough guy." Deep voice. "I got hit in the nose once." Big, warm hand on my shoulder. "With a baseball bat."

He's touching me.

"You guys remember that? The game against Everett Tech?"

He's actually touching me.

For a second, I feel no pain.

Stella? It's me, Evyn. Can you see my nose? My shnoz, *I should say.*

Tonight, Stella looks down at me, concern in her eyes. She reaches out a hand of comfort. *Oh, honey.*

It's okay, I tell her. *I only have to wear the splint for a week. And anyway, it was worth it. Linus gave me a piggyback to the car. Did you see that? Did you see him touch me on the head when we said good-bye? It was completely worth it.*

Stella smiles, nods. She understands.

Hey, Stell?

She raises her eyebrows — red-gold, like her hair. *Go on,* is what she means.

Did you wear a garter when you married Birdie? I never even heard of garters until today, and it made me wonder. Also, what did you wear that was old and new? Who did you borrow from? Which part had blue on it?

Suddenly, I want to know every detail about her wedding day. About marrying my dad. And about boys in general.

I want to be able to ask a million questions and have her answer every single one. And when I need advice, I want her to give it to me for real.

Not just in my imagination.

CHAPTER EIGHT

In the morning, I walk to the bus stop with Phoebe. I'm wearing new socks (diamond pattern) and shoes (black, chunky).

When I told Birdie I needed a fashion overhaul I thought he would hand me a five spot and send me down the street to CVS for a two-pack of knee-highs. What I did not expect was him broadcasting my private business to everyone in the house. What I did not expect was Eleni whipping out her wallet and saying why don't Clio, Cassi, Evyn, and Evyn's giant throbbing shnoz pop over to Copley Plaza for some shopping — her treat?

Half an hour later I was in the middle of Jasmine Sola, trying on platform heels while the sweater twins fought over the last pair of purple fishnet stockings.

That is why this morning I am walking to the bus stop in the right socks and shoes. *Put a bounce in your step,* Stella says. So I do. But I can assure you, that is not what people will be looking at.

When we get to the corner, Phoebe's friend Hannah gapes at me.

"Bear attack," I tell her, which was Birdie's suggestion.

"When in doubt," he said at breakfast, "use humor."

"When in doubt," I said back, "skip school."

But would he listen? No.

So here I am, traumatizing innocent first-graders at the bus stop.

"It wasn't really a bear, was it?" Hannah whispers.

Phoebe shakes her head. "My *brother* did it. With a *soccer* ball. They stopped the whole game and *everything*. There was *tons* of blood. Only he didn't mean to, it was an accident. Right, Evyn?"

"Right," I say.

Cleanser Boy has been apologizing to me every hour for the past thirty-six hours. I don't know whether he actually means it, or whether his mom is making him do it, but before I left this morning he started in again. "I'm really, really sorry, Evyn. I hope you're okay."

"I'm okay," I said.

Hannah, however, is not.

"Your *eyes*," she says now, a great sorrow in her voice. "*Look* at them."

Phoebe nods solemnly. "That is what happens. When you break your nose. Your eyes turn *black*."

Hannah takes a step closer to me. "Did it hurt real bad?"

"Yes," I tell her.

"Ohh." She pats my arm. "I'm sad for you."

Phoebe pats my other arm. "I'm sad, too."

It's the kind of compassion only six-year-olds can give.

Then Hannah says, "*I* know, let's do Miss Mary Mack!"

And Phoebe says, "*O*kay! You want to play, Evyn?"

I shake my head. "You guys go ahead."

Soon they are chanting and patty-caking at warp speed.

They're giggling like a couple of nuts. This is what it's like, being six.

I wish I could be six today.

I walk into homeroom expecting the worst. When I sit down, I feel the eyes burning into me from all directions.

After ten minutes of staring at my desk, I summon the courage to look up, and when I do, the girl to my right is smiling at me. Not in a mean way, either.

I turn to my left, and there is another one.

Two smiles — from the same two people who ignored me all last week.

"You're Ajax Gartos's sister, aren't you?" the first one asks.

"Well," I say, "not exactly. We're —"

"No way!" the second one squeals. "Your brother is sooooooo petute!"

Petute? Um, what?

The girl in front of me whips around. "I was at the game on Saturday. I saw everything. Look at your *face.* Ajax must feel awful! His own sister."

"Yeah, I'm not really his —"

"He's your stepbrother, right? Didn't you just move in with them?"

"Um. Yeah. We moved a few weeks ago. From Maine? My dad's marrying his —"

"Ableson, Chelsea." The homeroom teacher, Mrs. Kilgallon, is taking attendance. But nobody's listening.

"No *way*," says a girl a few desks down. She comes running over. "You live with Ajax Gartos? What's he *like*? Does he like anyone?"

Suddenly, I'm surrounded.

I heard he likes Wendy Rhenes.

Nuh-uh. He likes Jana Benson.

Does he wear boxers or briefs?

Mrs. Kilgallon raises her voice. "A-ble-son. Chel-sea."

Oh, he is definitely a boxer man.

Erica Sussman said that Carli Meyers said that her brother Paul said that Ajax does a hundred push-ups every day at soccer practice.

Don't you love the name Ajax? I love the name Ajax.

"Girls!" Mrs. Kilgallon is mad now. She picks up a stapler and bangs it on her desk. "Sit! Down! Or you! Will get! Detention!"

Everyone scatters. The room is dead calm.

"Ableson, Chelsea."

"Present," says the girl to my right.

When Mrs. Kilgallon isn't looking, she leans over and whispers, "Hey. Sit with us at lunch?"

I smile. Ableson, Chelsea, smiles back.

The girl to our left, Jaime, smiles, too.

And miraculously, I forget that my face looks like roadkill.

For the rest of the morning, I feel like a celebrity. People stop me in the hall. They ask me how I'm doing, where I got my shoes, if I want a piece of gum.

At lunch, a table of headbands flags me down, and I go over. Each one is prettier than the next, and I know right away these are the It Girls — the ones everyone wants to sit with. And they saved a seat for me.

"Ajax Gartos is your brother?" they ask.

I nod.

They move their chairs closer, and I start opening my lunch.

"Your brother is the hottest guy at Thorne," I'm told by a girl with blond, wavy hair. Her name is Andrea, but it's pronounced On-DREY-a, and she is clearly their leader.

"We need to know things," Andrea says, opening my milk for me and sticking in a straw.

"Like who he likes," says another girl.

"And if he's going to the social next Friday," another pipes in.

"Is he?" asks a girl with shiny lips. "Going to the social?"

I have no idea. I don't even know what the social is. But I know what I'm supposed to say. "I think so. Yeah."

Little squeals of excitement all around.

Andrea nods. "Good. What else?"

Everyone is looking at me. Suddenly, I'm the one with the answers.

I have to come up with something good.

"Well," I say slowly, "he has a poster of that Russian tennis player on his wall. You know — the really pretty one with the braids?"

Andrea smiles. "He likes blonds."

"Uh-huh." I pause to take a sip of milk. "And he likes spicy food. And hummus."

All around me, heads nod. They want me to keep going, so I do. I tell them everything I know.

When the bell rings, Andrea stands up.

"Find out who he likes," she tells me.

I say I'll get right on it.

"You do that." She gives me a little pat on the shoulder, for encouragement. " 'Bye for now," she says, and I say, " 'Bye, Andrea."

As I walk away from the table, it occurs to me: The whole time I was sitting there, no one asked my name.

CHAPTER NINE

It's Thursday night, and we are having a "family meeting." This is yet another example of Birdie's new vocabulary — right up there with "quality time" and "sibling bonding." I call it Al-Speak, and it makes me want to yank out every hair on my head, one by one.

Now, Al is standing in the middle of the living room, holding something orange and folded.

"I have in my hands," he says, "a symbol of the collective journey we are about to undertake."

He looks around at us, squashed together on two couches, and his eyes stop on Eleni. "Would you come up here, please? My bride-to-be?"

Bride-to-be. Blech.

I try to catch Mackey's eye so I can make a face, but he is three Gartoses away, looking straight ahead.

"Al." Eleni is smiling. "What are you up to?"

It takes her exactly a nanosecond to be by his side — a midget, gazing up at a giant.

I don't know how either of them can stand it. I guarantee they're in for a lifetime of neck pain.

"Honey," I hear my father saying. "Kids . . ."

I'm not sure what's coming next, but I know I'm not going to like it.

"I'd like to introduce to you . . ."

If Linus was here, at least I could focus all my attention on him. But he has class tonight. Economics. *Econ,* he calls it. Which is so cute. Linus is always coming up with —

"The Gartos-Linney Utopian Experiment!"

The Gartos-Linney Utopian Experiment.

"Oh, Al! It's wonderful!"

Oh, God, it's a T-shirt. A construction-cone-orange T-shirt with ten sets of puffy white handprints encircling the planet Earth and puffy white lettering.

"Um, Al? Did you, like, make those?"

Ten construction-cone-orange, white-puffy-paint T-shirts.

"Yay! Can I bring it for show-and-tell?"

And we're supposed to put them on.

"We don't have to wear those outside, do we?" one of the twins asks.

But Birdie just laughs. He turns to Eleni and says, "Hon? Get the camera. We're making memories here."

I am in the back "yard" — the only place I could find that's Gartos-free. Clam is out here, too, banished by Eleni. Apparently, Thalia is violently allergic to pet dander. Whatever.

I go over to the doghouse Birdie built for him. In the old

days, Clam got to sleep with one of us, snuggled at the foot of our beds.

Now he gets carpet on top of cement.

"Hey, boy," I say, scratching his ears the way he likes it.

Usually, he wags his tail like crazy. This time, he just looks at me with weepy eyes.

Clam is so ugly. He is a pug-bulldog mix with a smashed-in face, and his life's ambition is to slobber and fart. As a rule I don't like to get too close to him, but tonight I hug his neck. I breathe in his disgusting wet-fur smell, tinged with dog doo, but it's also the smell of Maine — the ocean, and my old backyard, and Jules and Mackey and Birdie, and everything and everyone the way they used to be and never will be again.

I squeeze him harder, and he lets out a big whimper.

"I know the feeling," I say.

I never really liked Clam before. Tonight, I love him.

I'm going to talk to Mackey. He is only one step up from a dog, I realize, because he won't talk back. But at least he's human. And at least he knows Birdie as well as I do — maybe even better, since he is two years older. He has to be freaking out a little bit, too.

When I get to Mackey's room, I don't bother knocking. I can hear computer game sounds so I know exactly what he's doing. He's hunched over his keyboard, grinding his teeth, muttering curse words. Maybe I will play with him tonight, the golf game. That one's not bad.

But when I open the door, someone has taken my spot.

It's Cleanser Boy, sitting right there next to my brother, wiggling a joystick and pressing buttons like mad.

Mackey yells out, "Die, vile scum beast of Zelkor! Die!" and Ajax doesn't even blink, so I can tell he is into it, too.

This is sibling bonding at its finest, only I'm the one who should be playing. Even if it's not golf — even if it's dragon-related and I have zero interest — I am the actual sibling here.

"Mack," I say. "I need to talk to you."

But he just grunts, rising halfway out of his chair and yanking the joystick so his knight charges ahead.

"Mackey. It's important."

"Hold on," says Ajax. "Let me kill him first."

I want to say, *I wasn't talking to you, Cleanser Boy, I was talking to my brother.* But I don't.

I sit on the beanbag in the corner and wait.

"I can't believe you're still wearing that thing."

Mackey looks at me, and I can see the dragon-slaying ecstasy in his eyes. "What? It's just a shirt."

"It's not just a shirt," I say.

I can't believe he doesn't get it, because it's so obvious, and if I have to spell it out for him, then what's the point.

"Operation Glue," Ajax says.

"Ex*cuse* me?" I say.

He grins. "GLUE. It's an acronym. Gartos-Linney Utopian Experiment? Two families, *stuck together*?"

Mackey smirks.

"Whatever," I say, and start for the door. I don't want to be in here anymore. It's not helping. It's making everything worse.

I'm halfway down the hall when a hand taps my shoulder.

"Hey. Evyn. Are you okay?"

I whip around. "Yes! For the hundredth time. It's just a broken nose."

Cleanser Boy shakes his head. "No. I mean, are you okay? You seem bummed."

I don't say anything.

"Is it the wedding? Because, you know, it's weird for all of us. The thought of having a new dad . . . I mean, your dad's cool and everything, it's just . . . you know."

I stare at him. This is the most he's ever said to me.

"Yeah," I say. "I know."

"I haven't seen my dad in five years. Did Al tell you?"

I shake my head.

"It's true. One day he was here, the next he was gone. Packed up all his clothes and just took off. He said the 'parenting thing' wasn't for him. Direct quote."

"Seriously?"

He nods. "He has a new wife now, in Denver. *Tiffany.* Who's, like, nineteen."

"Oh . . . sick."

"Yeah. He used to call sometimes, on our birthdays. Not anymore, though. Now he sends money. Lots of money. Which is good, I guess. But it's not . . . you know —"

"Not like having a real dad."

Ajax nods. "Yeah."

"Huh."

For a minute we don't say anything.

I think about Stella. I think about how things would be different if she didn't die — if they only got divorced.

After a while I say, "At least you got to know him. I mean, you got eight years, right?"

He shrugs. "I guess."

"Well, that's seven more than I got. With my mom."

Ajax frowns. "Right. I *knew* that. Hey, I'm sorry, Evyn. That was . . . I shouldn't have said anything."

"It's okay."

He shakes his head. "No. I wasn't thinking."

"It's o*kay*. Really."

"Okay," he says.

The conversation seems to be over, so I start to walk away. But then I remember something. All week I've been looking for clues. A snippet of phone conversation (*"Andrea is so hot"*). A certain name doodled on the back of a notebook (*Ajax luvs Andrea, S.W.A.K.*). So far, nothing.

Maybe it's time I tried a new tactic. "Hey. Do you like anyone?"

Ajax looks at me. "What. Girls?"

"Yeah."

"At your school?"

"Yes, girls at my school. Do you like anyone?"

He smiles. "Who wants to know?"

"Do you always answer a question with a question?"

"Why? Am I annoying you?"

"Are you going to answer the question?"

"Do you want me to?"

I feel like I'm talking to the opposite of Mackey. Instead of no response I'm getting harassed. I don't know which is worse.

"Never mind," I say. "Forget I asked."

Ajax laughs. "No, I'll answer the question. . . . *Maybe*."

"*Maybe* you like someone?"

"Maybe I like someone."

"Are you planning to tell me who it is?"

"Nope."

"Are you planning to ask her to that social thing?"

"Nope."

"Well, are you at least *going*?"

"Maybe."

"Great," I say. "Thanks a lot. You've been incredibly helpful. Really."

Cleanser Boy grins. "Hey, if I'm going to be your brother, I have to start acting like it, right?"

"Whatever," I say, and start walking away. And I don't know why, but I'm smiling.

Even though he is incredibly irritating.

CHAPTER TEN

It's Friday morning, and I have Latin. Here are the rules when you're the only kid in class: You can't forget your homework; you can't space out; you can't draw doodles of Mr. Murray's bald head and copious arm hair and pass them around with captions that say *Mr. Furry: Lusus Naturae,* which is Latin for "freak of nature." All you can do is pay attention.

Mr. Murray is sitting on the radiator when I walk in. "*Salve,*" he says, raising one hand.

This is Latin for "whatsup." There is excitement in his voice. It's like he can't wait to start teaching me more dead words.

"*Salve,*" I say, politely getting out my notebook.

I don't know why I'm taking this class. I guess because in seventh grade, Latin was cool. At my old school, everyone signed up for it, not just the geeks. The teacher, Mr. Camp, wasn't like most teachers. We played Latin charades, acting out sayings like *In vino veritas* — "*In wine is truth*" — and he didn't even care that we were pretending to be drunk. Plus, he didn't believe in quizzes; he just had us conjugate out loud, as a group.

Now I'm on my own.

When Mr. Murray asks, "*Quo vadis* this weekend?" I have no choice but to respond.

"Um. How do you say *wedding* in Latin?"

"Ah."

Mr. Murray smiles and uncaps a dry-erase marker. Since there's no chalkboard in the Latin closet, he uses a miniature whiteboard, which he holds in his lap at all times. He calls it his *tabula rasa.*

"*Nuptiae, nuptiarum.* Feminine. A wedding."

Then he adds some other useless vocabulary: *mustaceum,* a wedding cake; *fax,* a wedding torch; *hasta,* a ceremonial wedding spear.

Yes. I am so sure that Birdie will be carrying a ceremonial wedding spear tomorrow.

"So," Mr. Murray says, looking up, "who's getting married? *Consobrina? Consobrinus? Amita? Matertera? Avuncul —*"

"*Pater,*" I say, before he can name every possible relative. "My *pater*'s getting married."

"Oh," he says, nodding. "Uh-huh." He puts the cap back on the marker.

Silence.

I guess there's no word for stepmother.

Awkward, awkward silence.

I look down at my notebook and pretend to be studying. Mr. Murray clears his throat a few thousand times.

"Well," he says finally. "*Omnia vincit amor.* Love conquers all. Yes?"

I don't say anything. I'm trying so hard not to throw up.

I need to transfer to Spanish.

*　　*　　*

When I get to the cafeteria, the It Girls look happy to see me.

"How's Ajax?" they say.

I put my backpack on the floor. I have to keep my lunch in its bag today, because it's something gourmet and embarrassing and it stinks.

"He's good," I say.

Andrea leans over and opens my milk. She sticks in a straw. Every time, she does this. I don't know why.

"What's the latest?" she asks as she scoots her chair closer, while everyone at the table looks at me with big mascara eyes. These girls are so different from my friends in Maine. I don't know how to act around them.

"Well," I say, "my Latin teacher is sort of a pita." I still don't know what a pita is; I can only hope I used it right.

"OhmyGod, you take *Latin?*" This from Chelsea Ableson, my homeroom buddy.

"Isn't Latin, like, *dead?*" asks a girl with dangly earrings.

"Um," I say. "Yeah, but I'm thinking of transfer —"

Andrea holds up her hand. "Latin helps with your S.A.T.s. We should all be taking Latin. Shouldn't we, girls? Evelyn here will probably get into Harvard. Won't you, Evelyn?"

Everyone nods in agreement.

It's Evyn, I want to say. *Not Evelyn.* But I don't dare correct her.

"So," Andrea says. "Did you find out who Ajax likes yet?"

"Almost," I tell her. "I should know for sure by Monday."

She smiles. "Good work."

Everyone else smiles, too.

Translation: I'm allowed to sit here until the bell rings.

The night before a wedding means you have to rehearse. Which means, in my case, tossing imaginary flower petals on the carpet as I march in time to the organ version of "Love Me Tender" by Elvis.

Phoebe is glued to my side, like we're field-trip buddies on our way to the aquarium. Behind us is Thalia. Followed by the sweater twins. Followed by Eleni, who is holding fake flowers but shedding real tears. The acoustics in this church are faaantastic. Everyone will be able to hear her crying for joy. She is just so head-over-heels in love with my father, she's overflowing.

I will not think about it. I will not think about it. I will not think about it.

I will look straight ahead and focus on the groomsmen. On one groomsman in particular, who tomorrow will be wearing a tux and looking beyond gorgeous.

Stella? It's me.

This time she has her head down so I can't see her face.

Stell?

She's never done this to me before — not responded. I give her a minute, but she doesn't look at me, so I start right in,

Can you believe tonight? Eleni and her whole "I never thought I'd love again and then I met Al" speech? I thought I was going to barf right there at the table. Of COURSE she had to cook for the rehearsal dinner instead of us going to a nice restaurant like normal people because it's all about HER. Have I mentioned how much I am beginning to hate hummus? I can't believe Birdie is actually going through with this. I can't believe I have to wake up in the morning and put on an orange dress and pretend to be happy, when —

Stella is looking at me now. Her eyes are red, but she is as beautiful as ever. *Oh, honey,* she says.

For a moment, all we do is look at each other.

You'll be there tomorrow, I say finally. *Right?*

She gives a laugh that is more of a hiccup. *You want me to come to my own husband's wedding?*

I nod. My throat is so tight I can't talk.

Stella fishes around in the pocket of her bathrobe. She comes up with a tissue and blows her nose hard. When she's done, she folds it and puts it back in her pocket.

You're not going to make me dance the chicken dance, are you? she says. *Because I really hate the chicken dance.*

You can sit that one out, I tell her.

She gives me a tiny smile. *In that case . . .*

She means that she'll be there tomorrow, and I'm so relieved that a million hot tears start pressing against my eyeballs, and there's nothing I can do to stop them.

Luckily, the sweater twins snore so loud, an armored tank could plow through the wall and they wouldn't wake up.

At least they won't hear me cry.

CHAPTER ELEVEN

In the limo, I'm squashed between Thalia and the bride, who has on a tan dress. Tan. Not that she should be wearing white; it's obvious she's no virgin, but come on. Tan?

There are no boys present, so the sweater twins feel free to say things like, "My boobs look like torpedoes in this," and "Crap. I think I just got my period," while Phoebe gets shifted from one lap to another, so no one will get wrinkled.

Now Thalia is breaking out the bobby pins. She wants to fix everyone's hair before we get there. I let her work on my flower crown, and she pokes me in the head a few times, trying to make it tighter. "This would be a lot easier if you had long hair," she says.

I look at her and think, *You don't know the half of it.*

For the rest of the ride, I close my eyes and pretend I'm on the beach.

At the church, we get escorted to a room with fluffy green couches and a big mirror. Eleni stands in front of it while everyone fusses over her. Thalia busts out the hairspray.

Phoebe goes to town with the hand cream. "You need to be *soft,* Mommy," she says, "when Al puts the ring on."

"Thank you, sweetheart."

As usual, the sweater twins are fighting.

"Pink lipstick? Are you kidding me? She's wearing earth tones."

"Well, we're not doing *orange,* Clio. We're not giving the bride *orange* lips. She'll look like a freak."

While I sit on a fluffy green couch the whole time, watching. Because I don't belong in here. If I should be anywhere right now, it's with Birdie, helping him tie his tie or something.

Then comes a knock at the door. "Ladies?"

The sweater twins go ballistic. "Oh my God!" They scream, running to block the door. "It's Al! Hide Mom!"

"You're not allowed to see the bride, Al!" Thalia calls out. "It's bad luck!"

He laughs. "I won't come in. I promise. I just need to borrow Evyn for a minute."

I go into the hall and lean against the door, staring at him. Birdie with no beard and no glasses, wearing a tux and shoes so shiny you can see yourself in them.

"You don't look like you," I say.

He smiles. "You don't look like you, either." Then, quietly, "You look like your mom."

"No, I don't."

"You do. With your hair pinned up like that? You look . . . you're beautiful, honey." His voice cracks when he says this.

I shake my head.

Birdie nods.

We're both silent, like we can't find the words.

Then he reaches into his pocket. "I have something for you. I've been wanting to give it to you for a long time. I was just . . . waiting for the right . . ."

He clears his throat and hands me a box, blue with metallic swirls, and I feel goose bumps all over my arms as I open it and take out a necklace.

"This was hers?"

Birdie nods. He motions for me to turn around.

I do, and he fastens the clasp. The pendant rests in the hollow of my neck — a silver teardrop shape.

"She would want you to have it," he says.

I turn again, and Birdie hugs me hard. He scruffs his chin against my scalp, and even though he's not scruffy anymore it feels good.

We stay that way for a while, until the minister comes up and puts a hand on my dad's shoulder.

"Albert," he says. "It's time."

Somehow, I make it through the ceremony part.

I smile. I toss petals like a pro. I stand at attention while Birdie and Eleni promise to love, honor, cherish, and blah, blah, blah. I even watch them kiss, without vomiting.

But when the minister says, "I'm delighted to introduce to

you . . . Mr. and Mrs. Albert Linney!" I can't fake it anymore, because I'm so mad.

Mrs. Albert Linney.

There's only one Mrs. Albert Linney, and that's my mom — the one whose picture has been hanging over the fireplace all my life, the one whose necklace I'm wearing right now. I don't care if she's dead, she's still a Linney, and Eleni's not.

Eleni Linney. It sounds ridiculous.

I watch Birdie take her hand and lift it in the air, like they just won a mixed doubles tournament. I picture a lifetime of baklava and family meetings.

I never thought I'd say this, but right now I hate my father.

At the reception, the only bright spot is Linus. Except that I can't get to him because he's surrounded by a million cousins, all flinging their boobs around, even though they're related to him and should know better.

I watch this from my seat at the kids' table, where Phoebe is trying to get me to draw something with our complimentary Crayolas. I want to draw a cliff and jump off it.

When it's time to cut the cake, the bride feeds the groom a sweet little bite and everyone claps politely. Personally, I prefer the tradition of smashing it in the other person's face. If the groom would do that right now, this could be the best wedding ever. But Birdie is too nice of a guy. There's not a cake-smashing gene in his body.

Out on the patio, I find Mackey. He is eating four-hour-old shrimp off some forgotten tray.

"Eleni Linney," I say. "Could there be a stupider name?"

"Lynn." Mackey dribbles cocktail sauce down his chin.

"What?"

"Lynn Linney. Lynnie Linney. That would be stupider."

"Okay, fine. But I still can't believe she took our name."

"Mmf."

"This has to be one of the all-time worst days of my life," I tell him.

Mackey shrugs. He grabs three shrimp and jams them all in his mouth.

"What. You don't think it bites?"

He shrugs again.

"You actually *like* her?"

Big swallow. "Eleni?"

"Yes, *Eleni.* She doesn't drive you crazy with her cooking and her smiling and her little comments? And the way she's all over Birdie all the time? That doesn't make you want to rip off your own fingernails?"

"Hrmp."

I stare at my brother. "Could you use some *words* for once? Some English?"

I can't look at him anymore. I can't watch him stuff his face or shrug like a moron. I can't try to figure out what he thinks about anything that matters.

I feel like my head is going to explode. I feel like if I don't get out of here I'll do something crazy, like smash cake in someone's face.

On my way out I pass the dance floor, where everyone is bouncing and sweating all over one another.

It's a combination of Eleni's friends (Roger? Clive! Petunia, yoo-hoo!) and her Greek relatives. Nobody from our side, unless you count Birdie's carpenter friend, Greg, or my great-aunt Janice, which I don't.

A slow song comes on, and I can't move fast enough. The last thing I need to see right now is the bride and groom making out.

I pick up the pace, weaving in and out of bodies, toward the door.

And then something amazing happens.

"Evyn?" There's a hand on my back. Big, warm.

I turn around. "Yeah?"

It's Him. With the tux. And the curls. And the shoulders. And the dream teeth.

And he
is asking
me
to dance.

Stella?
StellaStellaStella, are you watching this?
He told me to take off my shoes so I could stand on his feet.
And we're so close, my stomach is touching his stomach and I

*can smell him, and he smells so good, Stell, can you smell that?
It's like the sandalwood Birdie uses. I don't want this song to be
over. Is this what it was like, the first time you danced with
Birdie? Did you never, ever, ever want the song to end? Ever?*

Stella smiles at me. And for the first time all day, I
smile back.

CHAPTER TWELVE

On Monday morning, Birdie leaves for his honeymoon. They are going to Vermont, to a bed-and-breakfast. I can picture them eating breakfast just fine (fresh-squeezed orange juice and buckwheat pancakes with real maple syrup), but the other part — the *bed* part — is too disgusting to contemplate.

So I won't think about it.

Instead, I will think about the fact that for an entire week there will be no parents in this house. For an entire week, I can do whatever I want.

"Emergency numbers on the fridge," Eleni says. "Al's cell, my cell, the B and B, fire department, poison control . . . Food money here, in this envelope. That's *food* money, not *shoe* money, understand?"

Thalia nods. "Of course."

In loco parentis, Thalia is in charge. Which is a joke, because there's no way the sweater twins are going to listen to her.

But this morning everyone pretends. There are instructions about bedtime (reasonable) and TV watching (limited). Suggestions for outings we might take (How 'bout the zoo!), to foster stepsibling bonding. Reminders that the usual rules of the house apply.

Sure they do.

"And if there are any problems," Eleni says, going down the line, hugging everyone, "any problems at all . . . call Linus."

She is directly in front of me when she says this, so when I smile she thinks I'm smiling at her.

"Evyn, honey." She sandwiches my cheeks with her hands. "I hope you have a wonderful week."

"Uh-huh," I say.

"Love you." She's looking me straight in the eyes and still has me in a cheek-wich, so there's no pretending I didn't hear her.

But I will not say it.

I mutter *Okay* and wait for her to move on to Phoebe, who jumps into her arms and starts planting wet ones all over her face. "Muh! I love you, Mommy! Muh! Muh! I love you and love you and love you and miss you and miss you! Muh!"

I get a sick feeling in my stomach, watching them.

I look at Birdie. He opens his arms.

"Have a good trip, *Al*," I say, walking out before he can try to hug me.

On the bus, I think about the kinds of "problems" that might arise that would necessitate a call to Linus.

A clogged drain. A small stove-top fire. Clam getting his fat face stuck between the slats of the fence.

"Linus," I will say, "this is Evyn. You know, from the wedding? We danced to 'She's Always a Woman' by Billy Joel?

Anyway, we're having this little problem here at the house, and I was wondering . . ."

And he will say, "Of course, I'll be right over." Even though it might mean missing his poli-sci class. Or coming straight from the gym, in his shorts, with that good kind of guy smell wafting off him.

There is so much I want to learn about Linus, but I have to find it out carefully, bit by bit, because I can't be too obvious. If I reveal my true feelings too soon, I'll ruin everything.

It's like this. I know we're related, but we're not *really* related. We're not actual blood relatives. Our children wouldn't be born with webbed fingers or with an extra foot growing out of their back or anything like that. And I know we're six years apart, and that seems like a lot now, but what about when I'm twenty and he's twenty-six? Or eighty and eighty-six? We'll both have dentures by then, and applesauce running down our chins, so what would it matter?

For now, the trick is to show him that although I'm thirteen, there is more to me than just a number.

Much more.

As soon as I walk into homeroom, I am attacked.

"So?" Chelsea says. "Who is it?"

Crap.

"We've been waiting for, like, *ever* for you to get here!" says Jaime. "You found out, right?"

Double crap.

I have absolutely no idea what I'm going to say right now. But I can't let them know this. I have to give them something.

"Of course." Mysterious smile. ". . . I'll tell everyone at lunch."

"No *way,* you're going to make us wait?"

"But E-vyn, we're dying here."

Well, at least someone got my name right.

"Good things come to those who wait," I say, unzipping my backpack oh-so-casually. Meanwhile, every cell in my body is sweating.

I have exactly four periods to think of an answer.

At high noon, the It Girls are waiting.

Andrea has already laid out my napkin and utensils. There are a few extra chairs at the table as well, for the Almost-But-Not-Quite-It Girls, invited for the occasion.

Andrea waits for me to sit before she speaks.

"I understand you have some information for us."

The smile is laid-back. The voice is friendly. But there is absolutely no question as to what I'm supposed to say.

I look at Andrea and nod.

"And you're sure this information is correct?" she says.

"Yes."

"Well?" says a girl with bangle bracelets. "Who is it?"

I have no choice. I have. No choice. I wish I had a choice, but I don't.

"Um," I say. "Andrea. He likes Andrea."

Please God, let Cleanser Boy like Andrea.

"Me?" Andrea says, pointing to her chest with one finger. "He likes me?"

Like she's surprised.

"Yes," I say. "He likes you." I open my brown bag and take out the sandwich I packed for myself this morning. Baloney. Which, right now, I am full of.

The squeals are ear-piercing.

"No *way!*"

"I *so* bet he kisses you at the social."

"You are sooo lucky, Drey!"

"Well," Andrea says, lowering her gaze just a bit, "it could have been any one of us, girls. You know that. . . . Now, what's everyone *wearing*? Evelyn?" She smiles at me, kindly, like a queen might smile at her gnarled, hunchbacked lady-in-waiting. "What are you wearing to the social?"

What am I wearing to the social? I know one thing: I cannot possibly answer this question correctly.

"Um," I say. "I'm between outfits."

All around me, girls nod. They understand this dilemma.

Andrea pats my shoulder. Is this for sympathy or pity? I can't tell. Either way, she's moved on.

"I'm thinking of getting lowlights," she says, turning her back to me. "Lowlights are the new highlights."

A dozen headbands and ponytails bob up and down in agreement.

I find myself nodding, too. "You totally should," I say.

Andrea looks at me. "You think?"

"Totally."

I don't know who I am right now. Yes, I do. I am one of those annoying girls who say *totally*.

"Well, Evelyn," Andrea says, "I think I just might."

"Ajax will like that," I say.

She smiles. I smile.

She pats my arm. And I leave the cafeteria with a giant wrecking ball in my stomach.

When I get home from school, I call Jules.

"I don't know what to do," I say. "If Ajax doesn't like Andrea, I'm dead."

Jules snorts. "On-DREY-a? What kind of a name is On-DREY-a?"

"I have no idea."

"Well, she sounds like a jerk. Why do you care what she thinks? There have to be better people to hang out with."

I don't say anything. Jules isn't here. There's no way she can understand what I'm going through.

"I tried calling yesterday," I say, changing the subject. "Where were you?"

"Oh!" Her whole tone changes. "I was at the ortho. I got my braces off! Finally!"

She goes on to tell me all about her teeth, how incredible they look, and how this changes everything. Right now she is ninety-nine percent positive that Jordan Meyerhoff is going to ask her out.

"Jordan Meyerhoff?" I say. "Jordan *Meyerhoff*?"

"Yes!"

"But we hate Jordan Meyerhoff."

"I don't *hate* anyone." There is a little edge to her voice.

"He locked Jason Perry in a locker."

"Yeah, in *sixth grade*."

"He laughed when you got your period in gym class. He used to call you Snaggle Tooth."

"Well, now he calls me hot. People change, Evyn."

Yeah, I think. *They sure do.*

For dinner, Thalia orders pizza and chicken wings. I could kiss her for not cooking.

The one thing I don't like is how she makes us sit together in the dining room. I would much rather eat in the yard, with Clam.

"If everyone could look at me for a sec," Thalia says, "I have an important announcement."

I'm not interested in her announcements, important or otherwise, so I keep eating.

"Someone at this table is too modest to tell you himself, therefore I will have to tell you for him."

Everyone is quiet, and I have no choice but to listen. Even though I don't give a hairy hoot what incredible thing Ajax did on the soccer field today.

"Let us all raise a glass," Thalia says, "to Mackey . . ."

Huh?

"Or should I say *Joseph?*" Huge smile. "And his amazing technicolor dreamcoat!"

The sweater twins scream. They run around the table to hug my brother.

"No *way!*"

"Mackey, you got it? Oh my God!"

Phoebe jumps up and down, clapping.

"Way to go, man," Ajax says, thumping Mackey on the back. "That's really awesome."

I'm racking my brain, but I have no idea what they're talking about. Mackey's face is bright red, probably because the sweater twins are mashed up against him on both sides.

I must look confused because Thalia says, "He got the part. The *lead.* He's Joseph!"

"Oh," I say.

Now I remember. The dorky play audition.

I stare at Mackey. "You tried out? For a *play?*"

He shrugs. "Thalia can be very convincing."

"It's not actually a play," Thalia says. "It's a musical."

"*Joseph and the Amazing Technicolor Dreamcoat,*" says one twin. "It's famous."

And the other one says, "You didn't tell us your brother had such an amazing voice, Evyn."

Amazing voice? Mackey?

The truth is, I've never thought about it. I hear him singing sometimes, in his room, or when he's taking a shower, but it's always been like Birdie's whistling habit — annoying.

I don't think he's ever seen a musical in his life.

"Yes," I say, nodding. "Broadway has always been Mackey's

dream. Ever since he was a small child, he's had only one true love. The stage."

I stare at my brother, but before he can say anything, the phone rings. It's the honeymooners, checking in. As soon as they hear the big news, they're fit to bust.

Mackey has a look on his face I've never seen before. It's like he's trying not to smile but can't help himself.

"I know," he says to Birdie. "I can't believe it, either."

Here is my brother. On the phone. Speaking actual English and showing joy like a normal person.

All I can think is, *Who are you?*

Stella?

It's me, Evyn.

What is it with everyone around here? First Birdie, then Jules, and now Mackey. Nobody wants to be who they used to be anymore. They're all changing, and I hate it.

Why can't we go back to the way things were, when Birdie was Birdie, and Jules had the snaggletooth, and Mackey was just my dweeb brother, not Mr. Joe Broadway?

Stella half smiles, half sighs.

I can tell she doesn't have any answers for me tonight.

Her eyes say, *I'm sorry, honey.*

It's okay, I tell her.

Even though it's not.

CHAPTER THIRTEEN

We've been parent-free for five days now, and the house looks like a war zone. There are clothes and pizza boxes and crusty dishes everywhere, and even Thalia has given up trying to clean.

At breakfast, one of the sweater twins opens a Cheerios box, and all that's left is dust.

"Thanks a lot, you guys," she says.

The other one shrugs. "You snooze, you lose."

"Shut up, Cassi. What am I supposed to eat now?"

"I'll make you some toast if you want," Thalia says, opening the fridge. "Oh. We're out of bread."

"Great. That's just great."

Phoebe holds up a spoon, dripping milk everywhere. "Want some? I'll share."

"Yeah. I really want your backwash for breakfast."

"Don't be a pita, Clio. It's not Phoebe's fault."

There it is again, that word. The sweater twins know everything. I bet if they were in my class they would fit right in at Andrea's table.

"Shut up, Cassi."

Oh, they are so obnoxious, and one of these days I'm going to tell them off, but not today. Today I need them.

"Did you guys ever go to one of those social things?" I ask.

"Oh my God," they say. "Remember *socials?*"

Like they were in eighth grade twenty years ago.

"Is it tonight? What's the theme? Who are you going with? Are you crushing on anyone? What are you *wearing?*"

"I don't know," I say. "If you have any . . . um . . . fashion advice, I'd be open to —"

The sweater twins look at each other and flip out. "Makeover? Makeover? Makeover!"

"Well," I say. "If you want."

The school day crawls by. A girl named Clara Bing is my math partner. Clara Bing is short and has allergies like you wouldn't believe. On the rare day that she can breathe through her nose, she sounds like a train whistle. And her eyes are always watering. I know for a fact that the It Girls call her "Sneezy Dwarf" behind her back.

"Do you remember how to convert this?" she asks in her froggy voice. "I always forget what to divide by."

"Me, too," I say. "I stink at math."

She wipes her nose with a tissue and smiles. "Me, too."

After a while I say, "Are you going to the social tonight?"

She shakes her head. "I don't go to those things."

"Why not?"

"I just don't."

"Why?" I keep on her. "Did you ever go to one?"

"Once. Last year. It was like . . . I don't know. All the guys on one side of the room, all the girls on the other. Nobody really dancing, except for slow songs when it's like *couples only*. It just wasn't that fun."

"Oh," I say. "I see."

And I do. Clara Bing is not the kind of girl who gets asked to dance. She doesn't know what it's like to have your stomach pressed up against someone else's. Or to smell his smell. Or to feel his hand, warm against your back. She doesn't know what she's missing.

"If you want," she says now, "you can come to my house tonight."

I look at her. "Why?"

"Every Friday, we rotate. Tonight's my night to have the girls over. The Four-Foot-Two Crew." She smiles. "Because, you know, we're all short? Anyway, we watch movies. Eat crap. Engage in actual dance moves. If you want to come . . ."

"Oh."

I picture a room full of midgets with watery eyes.

"No," I say. "Thanks. I'm going to the social."

Clara Bing nods and pulls out another tissue. "Okay. Well, the offer stands."

"Sure."

When the bell rings, she says, "Have fun tonight, Evyn."

"Yeah," I say. "You, too."

Makeover? Makeover? Makeover!

I barely recognize myself. I have on two colors of eye

84

shadow. I'm wearing leather pants. I don't know what kind of goop they put in my hair, but it actually looks good for once — like something out of a magazine. *Punky,* Clio called it. They covered up my bruises and made my nose look halfway normal. And I have on Stella's necklace, for luck. So, although I'm not getting my hopes up, I have to say it. Tonight I feel the tiniest bit like Cinderella.

Even Cleanser Boy notices. "Hey," he says on our way to the car. "You clean up nice."

"Thanks," I say. "You, too."

He does. In a preppy, jock-boy sort of way. But whatever he put on for cologne is horrifying. Especially in an enclosed space. As soon as we get in the car, I open my window.

Thalia is driving. She is in full substitute-parent form — tossing out little public service announcements the entire ride.

Remember, kids, you don't have to be high to have a high old time. And *Cigarettes won't make you look any cooler.*

Ajax laughs. "Our teachers are going. You really think they'll be serving up martinis and matches?"

"I was in eighth grade once," Thalia says. "I know what happens at these things. I just don't want you to do anything stupid."

She looks at us in the rearview mirror. "Got it?"

Ajax raises one fist in the air. "Take a Stand for a Drug-Free Land."

I place a hand over my heart. "Count on Me to Be Drug-Free."

"Good," Thalia says. She pulls up to the curb and says she'll be back to get us at ten.

Ajax lets out a groan. "Ten? Come on. It ends at eleven."

Thalia turns around and smiles. "Sisters: The Anti-Drug."

The Thorne School for Boys looks exactly like the March School for Girls. Only the smell is different, like mayonnaise and feet.

About fifty people are gathered in the gym, and I can see that Clara Bing was right. Nobody's dancing. All the girls are standing in little clumps against one wall, whispering to one another, while the boys are on the other side, stuffing chips into their mouths.

One look around and you can tell the decorating committee didn't exactly break a sweat. There aren't any streamers or balloons or anything, just a couple of lame signs.

THORNE FALL SOCIAL:
PLAY THE ARCADE, DRINK LEMONADE.

HEY MARCH GIRLS,
DANCE YOUR SOCKS OFF,
BRING YOUR XBOX.

Xbox.

A video-game theme. This is how they impress us.

Mackey would be thrilled.

In the bathroom, Andrea is surrounded by the usual

headbands. But there seems to be a new fashion trend tonight: braids. Also, tennis dresses.

They're all staring at themselves in the mirror. When they put on mascara, their mouths make little pink O's of concentration.

Andrea sees me. "Hi, Evelyn," she says, but she doesn't turn away from her reflection.

"Hi," I say.

"Is Ajax here?"

"Yeah." My tongue feels like sandpaper.

"In the gym?"

"Uh-huh."

"Good." Andrea smoothes on some lip gloss and smacks her lips together. She hands her purse to a girl in a pink tennis dress and spins around. "Ladies?"

She says this and everyone snaps to attention. She walks out the door and everyone follows.

By the time we get to the gym, music is blaring. But still no one is dancing.

The boys have migrated from the snack table to the "arcade" at the far end of the gym. It is a sad sight — only three games, and one of them is pinball.

On the bleachers, most of the boys are playing handhelds by themselves, which they could be doing in their own living rooms. I notice that Ajax isn't playing anything. He's standing in center court with a bunch of other eighth-grade boys, doing what they do best: stealing one another's hats, punching one another's shoulders, burping. I watch them for a while, sickly fascinated. They can't stop moving for a second. They have to be hitting one another, or dodging out of the way, or grabbing their crotches at all times.

One of them has his hands down his pants at this very moment, making *adjustments*.

Eighth-grade boys are gross. It's a wonder girls want anything to do with them.

Was Linus like this when he was their age? I can't imagine it. He's so much cooler than they are. Not to mention more civilized and a better dresser. He's someone who understands not to use an entire bottle of cologne in one sitting.

Next to Linus, these guys are babies. I can't believe I wasted my makeover on them.

Over by the DJ booth, Andrea and her friends are crowded around, and I know exactly what they're requesting.

Can you, like, play something slow?

And the DJ nods and fiddles with his headphones and presses a few buttons, and something slow and cheesy comes on and every air molecule in the gym shifts.

You don't just feel the energy mutation; you can see it.

Slow song . . .

One by one, the boys put down their video games.

Slow song . . .

They remove their fingers from their noses and wipe them on their jeans and begin the painful shuffle across the gym floor to where the girls are waiting.

I don't know if anyone's planning to ask me to dance, and I don't care. Right now I have bigger things to worry about. Like which girl Cleanser Boy is walking toward.

I can't look.

I make a beeline for the pinball machine, which has been deserted.

I yank the spring loader and watch as my little silver ball flies up the chute.

Whizzzz!

I don't see Ajax walk over to a clump of girls.

Ping!

A clump of girls who are definitely not wearing tennis dresses.

Ping! Ping!

Or braids.

Ping! Ping! Ping!

I don't see him stop in front of Maya Glassman, who is on the soccer team and pretty — in a freckly, girl-next-door sort of way — but definitely not in Andrea's league.

Ping! Ping! Pingpingping!

My ball bounces around like crazy, and I am flipping the little flippers, trying desperately to keep it from falling into the ditch. So I don't see Ajax lead Maya out onto the dance floor and put his hands on her shoulders and steer her around in the slow box that seems to be the signature dance move of all eighth-grade boys.

Pingpingpingpingping! . . . Pingpingpingpingping!

Ten thousand points! Bonus round!

For the first time ever, I understand why Mackey is addicted to video games. Even though pinball isn't exactly a video game, and there aren't any dragons involved, I get it.

As long as you're playing, you can pretend that whatever's going on in the world around you . . . isn't.

I'm in the hall, getting a drink at the water fountain, when I find out what happened on the dance floor.

"Maya *Glassman*? What the hell? She's not even hot." The voice is Andrea's. There's no mistaking it.

I am frozen in place, water dripping down my chin, while the It Girls around the corner get louder.

"You're way hotter than Maya *Glassman,* Drey."

"Way hotter."

"Way."

"I can't believe he slipped her the *tongue*."

"Right there in front of, like, the entire *universe*."

"That lying little wench."

Andrea again. And this time I know she's not talking about Maya Glassman.

Let the slaughter begin.

On a bench outside the Thorne School, I call Jules.

One thing I can be thankful for tonight: Thalia gave us a cell phone, *for emergencies.*

Well, this is an emergency.

"Mrs. Anthony?" I say. "It's Evyn."

"Evyn Linney. What a nice surprise. We miss you, sweetheart. How's everything? How's Boston?"

Normally, I would take the time to chitchat. But tonight is not normal. Tonight, I need my best friend.

"It's okay. Can I talk to Jules?"

"Oh, sweetie, I'm sorry. She's not home. She's at a party."

"A party?"

"Mmmhmm. At Jordan Meyerhoff's house. You remember Jordan. From the football team?"

"Uh-huh," I say.

Mrs. Anthony makes a cooing noise. "Such a handsome young man. And so polite. He seems to have taken quite a shine to Julia. . . ."

I think about telling her the truth about Jordan Meyerhoff — that he's the biggest tool in the toolshed, and she'd better go pick up her daughter right now, before something bad happens.

But somehow I don't have the energy. Somehow, all I want to do is collapse on this bench and cry.

Stella? It's me, Evyn.

Did you hear what they were saying about me? Do you know what they're going to do to me?

Now the tears are flowing.

Oh, honey, Stella says. *Don't cry.*

For the first time ever, I get mad at her. *That's all you can* come up with? *"Don't cry"? That's the best you can do? You can't do any better than that? Thanks, Stella. Thanks a whole lot.*

Stella shakes her head. *You can't let those girls get to you.*

Right, I say.

She ignores my sarcasm and keeps going. *Whatever they call you, just tell yourself, "I'm rubber, you're glue. Whatever you say bounces off me and sticks to you."*

I stare at her. *What is this, first grade?*

Stella smiles. *Hey, it works.*

Right.

Let's try one, she says. *Call me something.*

What?

Call me something. Something mean.

I roll my eyes.

Humor me, honey.

Fine, I say. *You're a horrible mother.*

Again, she smiles. *Bounce!*

Your advice is for crap.

She smiles wider. *Bounce!*

And I'm glad you're up there instead of down here because if you were here I would hate you. . . . I DO hate you.

Bounce! Bounce! Bounce! . . . See? Stella says. *Not a dent.*

She looks down at me, and her eyes are warm and soft, even though the things I said to her were beyond harsh.

I know I'm supposed to say I'm sorry, which is what a good daughter would say to her dead mother right now. *I'm sorry, Mom, and thank you for giving me the tools to cope in this cold, cruel world.*

But I don't feel sorry — I feel mad. At everyone.

Mad at the sweater twins for dressing me like this. Mad at Ajax for dancing with Maya Glassman instead of Andrea. Mad at the It Girls for being so brutal. And at Jules for not being home when I need her, and at Mackey for never listening to a word I say, and at Birdie for falling in love and moving us here without asking and for morphing into someone I don't even know anymore. Mad at Eleni most of all.

It's not you, I tell Stella.

She smiles. *I know it's not, honey.*

I don't really hate you.

I know.

You must hate her as much as I do. Probably more. You hate her guts, don't you?

And Stella says, *Hate is a strong word, Evyn.* She gives me a little lecture on the Golden Rule and deliberate word choice. Then she sighs. *Yeah. I hate her, too.*

Just like I knew she would.

CHAPTER FOURTEEN

I am in bed feeling sorry for myself when I smell something. French toast, I think. Also bacon. Part of me wants to eat, but the part that remembers last night doesn't want to move. Ever. Staying in bed for the rest of my life sounds like a good plan. I can finish eighth grade through one of those Internet correspondence courses and never go to school again. I can forget everything that happened.

"Oh my God. How was the *social*?"

Unfortunately, the sweater twins aren't going to let me.

"Did you get, like, a million compliments on your hair? Who did you dance with?"

"Did you hook up with anyone? Was there alcohol?"

From their loft beds, the two of them are staring down at me. They have matching mascara rings around their eyes, like raccoons. And matching bed-heads.

For a second I think about telling them what really happened, how in one evening I managed to 1) wear the completely wrong thing, yet again, 2) get asked to dance exactly zero times, and 3) incur the wrath of the most popular girl in school. For a second I wonder if maybe they'd have some advice for me — a smackeral of "sibling support" in my time of need.

But then I remember who I'm dealing with — the people who dressed me.

"Remember in eighth grade when Vinny Petrizzo spiked the punch with vodka and Jocelyn Weintraub puked all over Mr. B's shoes?"

I wouldn't tell them the truth in a million years.

"It was awesome," I say. "I got totally wasted and kissed the soccer team."

In stereo: "The whole *team*?"

"Well," I say, "not Ajax. Obviously. That would be disgusting. But everyone else."

Oh, I wish I had a camera right now. The looks on their faces must be captured.

Our stepsister is out of control.

It's hard to tell if they're horrified or proud. Either way, they have been rendered speechless, which is reason enough to celebrate.

I think I will eat after all.

I walk into the kitchen in my pajamas — flannel, with tiny horses and hay bales on them, circa sixth grade.

I walk into the kitchen with gel spikes on my head and pillow creases on my face and morning breath from the tenth circle of hell.

I walk into the kitchen and
there

he

is.

"Hungry?" he asks.

I can't believe I'm wearing horse pajamas.

"I made the mother lode of French toast."

I can't. Believe. I'm wearing. Horse pajamas.

"You want o.j.?"

What I want is a toothbrush.

And a comb.

And the power to turn back time so I can run upstairs and start the morning over again, wearing a tube top and dark-wash jeans.

I don't say anything. I'm afraid to open my mouth.

But then Linus pulls out a chair and pats it, and I sit down at the table next to him. Suddenly, I can imagine a million mornings like this one, where we will wake up and eat breakfast together, and it won't matter what I'm wearing because what we have goes beyond the superficial. What we have is the real deal.

So what if the sweater twins are here right now, running their motormouths? So what if Cleanser Boy — who very likely ruined my entire school year by asking Maya Glassman to dance — is stuffing his face with bacon? All I am thinking about is Linus. Linus Gartos, whose fingers are long and beautiful as he spatulas another slice of French toast onto my plate.

I could stay in the kitchen like this forever. The air is warm and smells like syrup. On the radio: soft rock. There is no On-drey-a. No honeymooners. There's just Linus and me, and right now that's all that matters.

Later on, we play cards — baby games like Crazy Eights and Old Maid because of Phoebe.

When it's my turn, Linus hands me the deck and our fingers touch.

"Your deal, tough guy," he says, winking.

Tough guy. Our private joke. Only someone whose nose has been bashed could understand.

Somehow I manage to shuffle without dropping any cards. I even try the waterfall.

"Sweet moves," he says.

And I say, "Plenty more where that came from."

He smiles, and I smile, and I ask him to cut the deck, and he does, and now our fingers are touching again.

I could definitely get used to this.

CHAPTER FIFTEEN

Sunday morning. The honeymooners are back. Eleni bursts through the door calling, "Kiiiids! We're hoooome!" It's obvious she thinks we're the Brady Bunch and should all be lined up on the stairs in exact height order, big TV smiles plastered on our faces.

I stay where I am on the couch, stuffing myself with Oreos, my dirty sneakers propped up on the coffee table.

I listen to Birdie say, "Well, the place is still standing. That's a good sign. I don't smell any smoke. . . ." and Eleni laughs like a hyena, and then Phoebe comes charging down the stairs. "Mommyyyyyy!"

By the time they make it to the den, everyone is crowded around, asking questions about their trip. Stupid ones.

How was the drive? Was the foliage beautiful?

Did you mountain bike?

Did you have room service for, like, every meal?

(It wasn't a hotel, Clio — duh — it was a B and B.)

(Shut up, Cassi. B and B's have room service, too.)

So, was it, like, the most romantic week EVER?

Did you white-water raft? Did you bungee jump?

Did you miss me? I missed you, Mommy. I missed you, Al.

Did you miss me?

Linus isn't with them (weep, weep). He had an exam to study for. But Mackey is, and although he hasn't opened his mouth yet, there he stands, right smack in the middle of it all.

"Hey, Mack." Birdie throws an arm around him. "Congrats."

"Or should we be calling you *Joseph* now?" Eleni smiles with every tooth. "To help you — what is it they say in the theater? *Get into character*?"

Mackey turns red and mumbles something I can't understand.

Then Thalia pipes in. "Miss Mundt — she's the stage manager? She says that the musical director, Mr. Soderberg, says that Mackey is the most talented high-school tenor he's ever worked with. At the first rehearsal, everyone was completely blown away."

Now comes a run-through of everyone else's triumph-o'-the-week.

Phoebe: Outstanding-plus in capital letters.

Cleanser Boy: Two goals, four assists.

Sweater Twin #1: Asked out by Kevin O'Reilly. Yes, THE Kevin O'Reilly.

Sweater Twin #2: Remember that skirt she wanted? The purple suede one with the fringe? It finally went on sale — forty-five percent off. So she bought it!

Thalia: Finished her application essay for Williams, and it's good. Really, really good.

Betty Boop claps every time. "Way to go!" she says. "Good for you!"

Meanwhile, Birdie has worked his way over to where I'm sitting and is trying to butter me up. "Hey, Ev. Make some room for your old man, huh?" He goes in for the hug-'n'-head-scrub routine, like nothing has changed between us. "Missed you, kiddo."

"Uh-huh." I grab another Oreo, twist it open, scrape out the creamy middle with my teeth.

"Evyn!" Eleni notices me for the first time. "How was your week? How was school? How was the social? How was —" She stops and claps one hand over her mouth. "Errrm."

Birdie leaps up. "Honey?"

"Errrrrm."

"Again?"

Eleni nods wildly. Then she claps the other hand over her mouth and hightails it out of the room.

Of course, Birdie is two steps behind her.

Phoebe whimpers. "What's wrong with Mommy?"

We can all hear the lovely sound of puke hitting hardwood.

"Stomach bug!" Birdie calls out. "Nothing to worry about! Probably a twenty-four-hour thing!"

I twist open another Oreo and try not to smile.

I know I am a terrible person for feeling the way I do, because Eleni has never done anything bad to me, but I'm glad she's sick anyway. I don't know why it makes me feel good that she feels rotten, but it does.

Stella understands. She gets it, and she doesn't judge. Later, when I'm by myself, we will talk about it. Correction: I will talk, and she will nod along like she agrees with everything I say.

I *know*. I'm not delusional. I know that Stella is me, and I am Stella. I know that when I talk to her I am really just talking to myself. And I hate that I know that. Because knowing that reminds me that I am completely alone.

CHAPTER SIXTEEN

Monday morning begins with a deep freeze. In homeroom, Chelsea and Jaime talk over me like I'm not here. It's just like the first week of school, only this time I'm not invisible. This time I'm prey.

I busy myself with my assignment book and try to ignore their conversation, which is about as subtle as a sledge-hammer.

"Can you believe *some people* had the nerve to come to school today?" Chelsea says.

Like I had a choice.

And Jaime says, "*Some people* should think about trans-ferring . . ."

Believe me, I have.

". . . 'Cause this is, like, an *all girls'* school, and some people obviously, like, *aren't.*"

Ouch.

Even though I know it's pointless, I touch Stella's necklace and say the word softly to myself. *Bounce.*

"I hear the Thorne School is looking for a new bulldog mascot. . . ."

Bounce.

"Ableson, Chelsea." Mrs. Kilgallon bangs her ruler on the desk. "Ableson. Chelsea."

"Present," Chelsea says.

There is now a strict no-talking-while-attendance-is-being-taken rule, so you would think it would stop there, but it doesn't. They just move on to other, more sophisticated forms of torture.

First on their list: the insult-disguised-as-extended-cough.

"Achchch*bulldog*chch."

Then, the slow-motion passing of a notebook across the aisle, with the billboard-sized message written in pink gel pen.

Who's your barber? Boys-'R'-Us?

You can tell they've put a lot of thought into this. They've planned it out to the tiniest detail, which is downright pathetic if you ask me. They had nothing better to do this weekend than to come up with ways to make fun of me?

They think they're being clever, when really their efforts are so feeble it's sad. *She has short hair and no boobs and a boy's name, therefore she must be a guy.*

Yes, that makes total sense! That's so logical!

OhmyGod, these girls are clearly, like, total airheads with, like, ten brain cells between them.

It's not as if I expected to be best friends with them. It's not as if I didn't know all along they were just using me to get to Ajax.

But that doesn't stop it from hurting.

*   *   *

When I get to the Latin closet there's someone sitting at my desk: a boy. Thin face. Brownish-orange hair. Glasses with chunky black frames — the kind that are so dorky they're almost cool.

Mr. Murray isn't here yet, so it's just the two of us. Me and this *Boy* at the March School for *Girls*.

"Ha-ha," I say. "Very funny. You can go back to Thorne now."

He looks up at me. "Um. What?"

"Let me guess. Andrea sent you. You're supposed to say something brilliant, like, 'Pardon me, is this the guys' locker room? Do you have a jockstrap I could borrow?' Well, you can save your breath. I get it."

"Um. I'm confused."

"Right. You have *no idea* what I'm talking about."

He clears his throat. "You're, um, Ajax Gartos's sister, aren't you? Um, Evyn?"

This shuts me up for a minute. He knows my name. How does he know my name?

"I'm, um, Travis. Travis Piesch."

"And I'm Evyn Plum."

"Actually, it's, um, I-E-S-C-H." He stands and holds out his hand to me, just as Mr. Murray bursts through the door. "*Salve, scholastici!*"

Scholastici. Students.

Plural.

Oh.

Mr. Murray looks around, frowning. "I asked for another desk to be brought in here, but I guess no one got around to it."

104

Oh, no.

"You don't mind sharing, do you? Just for today?"

Mr. Murray sees the look on my face and explains. Apparently, the Latin teacher at the Thorne School just quit, and because Travis Piesch was the only student, the Powers-That-Be decided to make an exception and allow a coed class for the first time in March-Thorne history.

Clearly, Mr. Murray is thrilled. Enrollment has doubled! We can do projects! Plays! Let's start with *Julius Caesar*!

I feel like an idiot. And feeling like an idiot means I can't look at Travis Piesch for the rest of the period.

Do you have a jockstrap I could borrow?

Sometimes I am so embarrassed for myself it's staggering.

I stand in the doorway of the cafeteria, holding the eggplant sandwich Birdie made for me because Eleni was still barfing this morning. I watch Andrea and the other It Girls laughing together and eating their sugar-free, fat-free, and carb-free lunches. I wonder how they would react if I walked over.

I think of the different approaches I could take.

Sincere: *I'm really sorry I lied to you, Andrea. I know it was wrong, and I apologize. I just wanted to be friends with you guys.*

Breezy: *Welp, I guess Ajax moved on from tennis babe lust to soccer babe lust without informing me. You know how guys are.*

Humorous: *Hi, I'm Devyn — Evyn's twin sister? Can you believe what a loser she is?!*

But as I start to walk over, one of Andrea's clones glares at me, and her mouth forms a word I've never been called before. Ever.

My eyes tear up. My whole body stiffens. I couldn't bounce if my life depended on it.

I stand in the middle of the cafeteria, frozen. I literally can't make myself move from this spot.

I don't know how much time has passed. Ten seconds? Ten minutes? Ten years? All I know is I look like the biggest loser in the lunchroom.

No, you don't, Stella says.

I picture her smiling at me from a table near the door. She holds up her watch. *See? It hasn't been that long.*

See? I say. *The It Girls. They're all staring at me. Staring, whispering, giggling —*

Don't think about them, Stella tells me. *Just walk.*

I imagine her hand on my back, propelling me forward. *Put a bounce in your step, honey.*

When I get home, Eleni is M.I.A. Birdie is in the kitchen, and he's banging around the pots and pans, which is a bad sign. From the past thirteen years, I can tell you there are only three things my father can cook that are remotely edible: spaghetti, hamburgers, and soup from a can. Mackey and I are used to it, but this is Casa Gartos, where everything is gourmet, and I just don't see Bean 'n' Bacon à la Birdie going over well.

"What are you *doing*?" I ask.

Birdie looks up. "Making dinner."

"*Why?*"

"Eleni's still under the weather, so Chef Bird is on duty." He lifts the lid off a pot and stirs.

I know when I ask him what he's making he'll say something like Rice-A-Roni, alphabet soup, and home fries, and when he does I will say, *Are you crazy?* And he'll say, *What?* And I'll say, *Rice, pasta, and potatoes in one meal? That's disgusting. Nobody's going to eat that.*

But this is not what happens.

When I say, "What are you making?" Birdie smiles. He gestures to one pot after another. "Chicken cordon bleu. Green beans Florentine. Potatoes au gratin . . . You like?" He opens the oven door. "Tollhouse pie. From *scratch.*"

He looks so proud of himself, standing there in one of Eleni's aprons — white with pink roses.

I know he expects me to be impressed. He expects me to get all wide-eyed and say, "Wow! Smells fantastic! Can't wait to chow down!"

But I can't bring myself to do it.

"Suddenly you can cook?"

Birdie looks at me. "What?"

"Mackey and I get crap from a can our whole lives, and now — now that you have a new family — suddenly you can cook a four-course meal? For *them?*"

The smile slides right off his face. "I made this for everyone."

"Sure, *Al.* Sure you did."

I run through the kitchen and outside to the non-yard. I run straight for Clam. I hug his neck and breathe in his Maine smell and stay that way for a long time.

Later, I go to talk to Mackey, but when I get to his door it's not computer games I hear, it's singing. Real singing. It can't possibly be my geek brother in there, but it is. I try to picture Mackey up on stage, sweeping around in his dreamcoat, bowing dramatically for the crowd, but I can't. It just doesn't make sense.

Nothing makes sense.

I'm out in the yard again when Birdie comes looking for me. He puts a tray down on the grass — everything he made for dinner. It actually looks good, and I'm starving, but I won't touch it. I can't. Eating his food would be like saying I forgive him.

Birdie pulls up a lawn chair next to me. "Are you okay?"

I stare at Clam's water bowl.

"Ev . . ."

Big cloud of quiet.

He doesn't know what to say to me. Birdie — my own dad. Never in my life has Birdie not known what to say to me. We have always been able to talk. Even about embarrassing stuff. Bras. Periods. When I got my period for the first time, Birdie was the one who bought me pads. Birdie was the one who took me out for ice cream to celebrate. My friends couldn't believe it. "Your *dad* took you? You went with your *dad*? You talk to your *dad* about periods?" And I remember feeling proud about it. "I can talk to my dad about anything."

Now there's only silence between us. Silence and chicken cordon bleu.

After a while, Birdie looks at me. "This isn't about the food," he says quietly, "is it?"

I don't know what to say to that. He's right. This isn't about the food.

I want to say it. I want to say it all out loud, but how can I? Ever since he told us we were moving, he's been happier than I've ever seen him. How do I tell him that I can't stand the woman he married? That I never asked to be anyone's step-sister? That what I want more than anything is to go back to Maine, to my old house and my old friends and my old school, where I didn't have to work so hard to fit in?

I want to say it, but I don't want to hurt him. And anyway, what would be the point? It wouldn't change a thing.

So I take a bite of pie instead.

And it's good. It's so good I have to spit it back on the plate.

CHAPTER SEVENTEEN

Okay, it's official. I have been traumatized for life.

Why, on a Tuesday afternoon, was Eleni home at all? Why — today of all days — did I decide to use the peachy bathroom instead of the one downstairs? Huh? Isn't my life messed up enough already, without me having to experience what I have just experienced?

Let us recap.

I come home from school, needing to pee.

I toss my backpack on the kitchen table, grab a fistful of grapes from a bowl (starving, after yet another lunch period spent in the bathroom), and sprint up the stairs.

I throw open the door to the bathroom and . . .

Ahhhhgggggghhhhhhhhhhhh!

Flesh.

"Oh! Evyn, honey. We didn't know you were —"

Wet, steaming pink flesh.

"— home. . . ."

And hair. Oh, the hair.

Achhhhhhh. A grape lodges itself in my throat, from the horror of it all.

"Ev?" His voice.

"Honey? Are you okay? Are you choking?" Her voice.

Achhhhhhh!

And then.

Are you ready for this?

It's not Birdie who leaves the shower and comes to my rescue, it's *her*. *She* leaps out of the shower. Leaps, like a superhero. "I know the Heimlich!"

And does she have the decency to throw on a towel? No.

Warm, moist arms grabbing me from behind.

"Don't worry, honey!"

Boobs, mushing into my shoulder blades. Fists, jamming into my rib cage.

"I've done this before!"

Jam! Jam! Jam!

Out flies the grape. It hits the edge of the sink and ricochets onto the floor, right next to my foot.

"Oh, thank God."

She hugs me. Full frontal, my stepmother hugs me.

"Thank God you're all right."

I. Am not. All right.

Jules can't stop laughing.

"Thank you," I tell her. "Thank you so much for finding my life hilarious."

"I'm (hahahaha) sorry. It's just (hahahahaha). Oh my God! HAHAHAHAHA! Your stepmother . . . gave you the nude . . ."

"Yes. We've established that."

I don't know why I called Jules. Well, yes I do. Jules is my best friend. When a person is having a tough time, and her only legitimate parent has taken on an entirely new personality, who does she turn to? Her best friend. Only lately, it's been harder and harder to find Jules when I need her. Today, when I called her house, her mom said she wasn't home. She was at Jessie Kapler's house.

"Jessie Kapler?" I said. "Are you sure?"

"Yes," said Mrs. Anthony. "You remember Jessie Kapler. From the cheerleading squad?"

Yes, I remember Jessie Kapler from the cheerleading squad. Jessie Kapler is the Maine version of Andrea — picture Andrea with hairspray and press-on nails — and she has always been wayyyy out of our league, friendship-wise. Jessie Kapler, who used to make fun of Raquel's accent and Ann's nose, who called them "The Two 'Tards," in front of everyone.

"Sure," I told Mrs. Anthony. "I remember."

That is when she gave me Jules's cell phone number. Because now, apparently, Jules has her own cell phone. Not that she bothered to tell me.

"Oh my God, you guys," Jules is saying. "Listen to this. Evyn's (hahahaha) stepmother (hahahaha) gave her the naked (hahahaha) . . . Oh my God . . . I can't breathe . . . HAHA-HAHA! Heimlich!"

In the background, peals of girl laughter. I have to pull the phone away from my ear, they're so loud.

"Thanks a lot, Jules," I say, when things have finally calmed down. "Thanks for being such a fantastic friend. Really. I don't know what I'd do without you."

"Evyn, come on. You have to admit it's funny."

"Is it now?"

"Yes!"

"No. It's not. It's not funny." My voice catches in my throat. "This is my life we're talking about, and you're supposed to be my best friend. *Efftees,* remember? Friends 'til the end?"

Jules is quiet for a minute. I can hear whispering and then giggling in the background.

"Yeah, um, Evyn? We're getting a little old for that, don't you think? The whole *best friend* thing . . . it's, like, juvenile, you know?"

"Juvenile," I repeat.

"Um, yeah," she says.

"I see."

It's total silence after that. There's nothing else to say. Any words that might have considered leaving my mouth a few minutes ago are now clinging to the back of my teeth.

Jules doesn't say anything more.

So I hang up, without even telling her good-bye.

As if that's not bad enough, Birdie tries to apologize. He finds me outside and walks right over to where Clam and I are sitting.

"Hey, Ev," he says.

I bury my nose in Clam's neck and say nothing.

"Sorry about earlier," he says. "About the, uh, shower scene. . . . We should have, uh . . . remembered to lock the door. But we weren't expecting anyone to, uh . . . walk in. And, uh, I think you're old enough and mature enough to understand that when two married people, uh . . ."

I lift my head and stare at him.

"That when two married people love each other —"

Ugh.

"It's only natural that —"

"Birdie."

"Making love is a way of expressing —"

"Birdie!"

"What?"

"Stop trying to explain it to me! God!"

He takes a breath and lets it out in one long, slow stream. "You don't want to talk about what happened?"

"No. Way."

"Okay," he says, and it's obvious how relieved he is. "I can respect that. I can respect your feelings about that."

I stare at him. *Since when?* I think. *Since when do you respect my feelings about anything?*

But I can't get myself to say it out loud.

Stella? It's me, Evyn.

Don't even bother because I know what you're about to say. "Bounce." Don't let what Jules says bother me. Don't let what Birdie says bother me. Don't let what Andrea says or Eleni says or anyone else says bother me. Don't let anything bother me. Just "bounce." Well, guess what? Bouncing is a crock. It doesn't work. And neither does talking to you about anything. So, I'm done. These little chats of ours are over. Finito. Kaput.

Stella looks at me, a little smile playing on her lips.

You think I'm kidding? I reach behind my head — fiddle with the clasp of her necklace until it comes loose. *See? I'm taking this off. I don't need it anymore. I don't need you anymore.*

She opens her mouth as if she's going to say something, but no words come out.

Later, when I'm lying in bed, there she is again. Green eyes watching me. Soft pink mouth opening and closing, opening and closing, like a fish.

But no words come out. Not a single one.

CHAPTER EIGHTEEN

After another day of dirty looks and not one person to hang out with after school, I open the mailbox. Usually there's nothing for me — my Maine friends just call and e-mail — but today there is.

I stare at the envelope.

Miss Evyn Linney and Mrs. Eleni Linney.

A sick feeling comes over me as I open it, and not just because the yellow-and-green-plaid card stock is nauseating to behold.

> *You are cordially invited to the 47th Annual*
> *March School Mother-Daughter Tea.*
> *Sunday, November Twenty-third*
> *at Two in the Afternoon*

Are they serious? Do they actually think she's my mother? And if they know she's not — if they know she's just the woman my father married — do they really think I'd want to drink tea with her, anywhere? The thought of walking into the March School on a weekend, for an afternoon of small talk and crumpets, is bad enough. But with Betty Boop by my side? Forget it.

Luckily, I'm the one who brought in the mail. She hasn't seen the invitation yet, and now she never will.

Birdie walks into the kitchen just as I'm stuffing the last shreds of yellow and green into the trash can.

"Hey, Ev," he says, not noticing a thing. "How was the day?"

"Fine," I say.

"School was good?"

"Uh-huh."

"Anything to share?"

I look at him.

He's got that eager-beaver look on his face, like he's been doing some inspirational reading. *How to Connect with Your Daughter in the Kitchen After School.*

"Anything?" he repeats.

I shake my head.

I've never seen him act this way around me. We used to just talk, like regular people.

"You'll be here for dinner, right?" he asks.

"Why wouldn't I be here for dinner?"

He laughs — a jolly *har, har, har.* "No reason. It's just Family Meeting Night, that's all."

Family Meeting Night.

Linus.

Linus will be here.

"If you could be at the table by six o'clock that would be great."

I shrug. *Whatever,* my shoulders say.

But that shrug is a lie.

Inside, my heart is playing the bongos. My brain is flinging open storage drawers, in search of the perfect outfit.

Family Meeting Night. I have on a black camisole and tight black jeans — castoffs from Jules. Also lipstick. It's the kind of ensemble that a girl with short hair and no curves whatsoever could actually look good in. Even sexy. Maybe. If you were to squint at her from a great distance.

I come to the table, hoping I won't say anything stupid — hoping my crush-blush will behave itself.

But when I get there, Linus's seat is empty. Apparently, he has a take-home exam due on Monday, and it's half his grade. He's not here, and for the dinner portion of the evening I'm devastated.

The knee slapper is this: I only *think* I'm devastated. I don't know real devastation yet. No one does. Not Mackey, not Thalia, not the sweater twins, not Ajax, not Phoebe. Real devastation won't hit us until after dessert. Until after we file into the living room. Until Birdie and Eleni are standing right in front of us, beaming like a couple of halogen lightbulbs. It hurts my eyes to look at them.

"Kids." My father slides his arm around her shoulders and squeezes. "We have an announcement."

They move closer to each other. Closer. Closer. So close, her head gets wedged under his armpit. While the two of them blather on, I think about the fact that only the thinnest layer of oxford cloth separates her head hair from his pit hair.

"Blah, blah, blah. We wanted to make absolutely sure. Blah, blah, blah."

Sweat is soaking through the fabric onto her scalp.

"Before we told anyone. Blah. Blah. Blah."

Instead of Pantene, her hair now smells like armpits.

"But we went to see the doctor this morning. Blah, blah, blah. And of course we wanted you to be the first to know. Blah, blah, blah."

Shampoo de B.O. Ha!

"We're pregnant!"

We're pregnant!

The words hit me like a soccer ball to the face.

We're pregnant.

We.

WE are pregnant.

The silence in the room is deafening.

Birdie is looking at me. He's looking for a reaction, but I don't have one because my facial muscles are paralyzed. They can't move a bit. And if they could, I don't know what they'd do. If my mouth could open right now, what would come out? *Noooooooo!* He's still looking at me, and I am still frozen.

"Mazel tov," someone says, breaking the seal of silence.

Mazel tov.

I look around and see that it's Thalia who said it. Thalia is getting up off the couch and walking over to Eleni, kissing her cheek. Then, kissing Birdie.

I can't believe what I'm seeing.

"Mommy's having a baby? When? Can I name it? Is it a

girl? How will you get it out? Can it live in my room? When Hannah's mommy had baby Jillian, Hannah got to —"

"You're *pregnant*? How are you *pregnant*?"

"So *that's* why you gagged when I lit up my incense."

"Did you have the ultrasound yet? Do you know the sex?"

They're all talking at once. Words are flying through the air like hail balls, and every one of them hurts.

I look at Mackey. He looks at me and shakes his head — in what? Disgust? Disbelief? I can't tell.

"We know this may come as a shock," Eleni says, "but we hope we'll have your support in the coming months."

Support.

"We hope you're as excited as we are."

Excited.

"We might have to do a little switching around, room-wise, when the time comes, but —"

"Because what, we're not cramped enough already?" Ajax sounds pissed. "Where are we supposed to put another kid?"

The room erupts again — voices getting louder and louder and louder — until suddenly I can't take it anymore. I have to get out of here.

Scrambling up from the couch, I step on Phoebe's foot and she yelps, but I don't stop to see if she's okay. I just run.

"Evyn?" Birdie calls after me. "Ev?"

"Let her go," I hear Eleni say. "She just needs time."

Time? She thinks I need time?

I run through the dining room.

What the hell does she know about what I need?

Through the kitchen.

I don't need time. I need . . . I need . . .
I don't know what I need.

I run into the backyard.

Over to Clam, who's asleep under a bush. I flop down on my belly, not caring about the dirt, just wanting to smell his smell.

We're pregnant!

I snake my way along the ground, scratching my face on the branches, until I reach his pudgy little body.

And as soon as I touch him, I know.

Because of course. Isn't this exactly what would happen now?

I remember when I was five and Mackey was seven, and we had a parakeet named Pete, and one morning we came downstairs for breakfast, and Pete was lying on the bottom of his cage, cold and perfectly still, and I cried for a week.

But tonight, the tears don't come. Instead of crying, I run to the back door and yell, "Clam's dead! Are you happy? Is everybody happy now?"

Then I grab a bunch of twenties from Eleni's purse and take off.

CHAPTER NINETEEN

I can't get the words out of my head.

We're pregnant.

We.

WE are pregnant.

"I need to get to Portland, Maine," I tell the lady in the ticket booth. She has on a Red Sox visor with a mushroom hairdo sprouting out the top.

"Yah can't get they-ah from hee-ah," she says, and at first I think she's making fun of me, doing the old Maine hillbilly routine, but then I realize it's how she really talks.

"This is Ahlington. You need South Station." She takes out a little map and points with a pen. "Change hee-ah, at Pahk Street. It's wicked easy."

"Thanks," I tell her.

"Shoo-ah."

It's my first time riding the T, and I am alone. Well, not technically. I'm packed in with hundreds of other people who all seem to be drunk and wearing Red Sox jerseys, but I don't know any of them.

"I hate that pitchah," says the guy who's pressed up against my back.

And his buddy, whose elbow is jammed into my solar plexus, says, "He's a pissah."

I lean my cheek against a pole that's probably swarming with salmonella and wonder why nobody at the March School talks that way. Or the Gartoses. They don't have the accent. Why? Because they're loaded?

"Yankees suck!" someone on the other end of the train yells.

The whole train starts chanting, *"Yan-kees suck, Yan-kees suck, Yan-kees suck, Yan-kees suck."*

And even though I don't want to, I think about Birdie. Because he grew up in New York, and he still has the Yankees cap he wore when he was a kid. Because he took me and Mackey to a baseball game last summer. It was only the Portland Seadogs, minor league, but still. The three of us ate peanuts and Cracker Jack, and ice cream out of tiny baseball cap bowls. Then, during the seventh-inning stretch, Birdie stood on the bleachers and sang "Take Me Out to the Ball Game" at the top of his lungs.

I picture him in his sawdusty overalls, bits of popcorn stuck in his beard, embarrassing the crap out of his children in public, and a wave of sadness hits me.

I want to go back.

"Pahk Street! Pahk Street Station next!"

I want to go back to that summer, to that baseball game, to that exact moment in time.

The subway slows. As the doors open, I feel myself start to panic. Because I can't decide which way to go.

Stella? It's me, Evyn.

I close my eyes and wait. All around me, bodies are moving.

Stell?

Nothing.

I have two choices, right? Go back to Al and Betty Boop and their love child, or go home to Maine. Home, where I no longer have a house. Where my best friend may or may not be my best friend anymore. Where —

"Pahk Street! Pahk Street Station! Change here for the red line!"

People are shoving past me, but I stay where I am, waiting.

Stella?

"Hey," someone says.

There's a hot blast of beer breath in my ear.

"Move it or lose it, sistah."

I wait another second, but Stella doesn't say anything. She doesn't even show her face. It's like she never existed.

So I get off the train, stumbling through a sea of elbows and Red Sox jerseys, and I feel so scared and alone I want to cry.

But I don't.

I just keep moving.

In South Station, I find a pay phone. I don't have a credit card so I have to call collect.

"Guess where I am," I say.

And Jules says, "Where."

"Guess."

"I don't know. The mall?"

"The train station!" I sound more enthusiastic than I feel. "I'm coming to visit!"

"What? When?"

"Now! I mean, I don't have a ticket yet, but there's a train that leaves at eight-forty. It gets in at eleven-something. Do you think your mom can pick me up? Or your dad?"

"Um."

This is her response. *Um.* Not *Oh my God, Ev, I'm so psyched to see you!*, but *um.*

"What?" I say. "You don't want me to come?"

"It's not that. It's just . . . it's Friday night."

"So?"

"So, I have, you know, *plans.*"

"What kind of plans?"

"Just this high-school party."

Just this high-school party, she says. Like she's been going to high-school parties all her life.

"So?" I say. "Your curfew's ten-thirty. Your mom can pick you up from the party and then she can —"

"Ev."

"What?"

"The thing is . . . I'm sleeping over at Jessie Kapler's, so, you know . . ."

So, you know. You're not invited.

"Oh," I say.

"I mean, I want you to come and everything, it's just . . . Hey, did you call Raquel? Or Ann? Maybe you could stay with one of them."

Right. Because now that Jules has Jessie Kapler, who needs Raquel and Ann?

I stare at the wad of sweaty bills in my hand. I think about what I could do at a train station with all this money.

"Or, like, you could come another weekend. . . . Ev?"

Who needs a ticket to Maine when you can get a *Seventeen*, gum, and forty scoops of Ja-makin' Me Crazy Fudge?

"Great," she says. "Now you're mad? Hey, it's not my fault I have plans tonight. You could have given me a little notice."

By this stage there is no point in explaining why I wanted to come in the first place — no point in telling her my whole life is falling apart. The conversation has already deteriorated.

"You're right." I laugh into the phone. It's the kind of laugh that comes out when nothing is the least bit funny. "Next time I'll give you *notice*. Next time I'll take out an ad in the *Portland Herald*. No, wait. I'll hire a blimp to fly over your house!"

I slam down the receiver before she can say anything. That's the great thing about pay phones, you can just hang up and walk out.

I make my way over to JB Scoops. Fifty-two flavors. Maybe I'll try them all. Maybe I'll eat until I'm sick, until I never want to eat ice cream again in my life. Until I *explode*.

It's not like anyone is here to stop me.

* * *

Ohhhhh, my stomach. I can't believe I just did that.

In the restroom mirror, my face looks warped and pasty. I splash cold water over it again and again. I rinse my mouth and spit. Rinse and spit, but my teeth still feel like they're wearing individual caramel-fudge sweaters.

I hate ice cream. I really do.

After that, I wander around. I find the escalator and ride it up and down a few times. When we were little, Birdie would take me and Mackey to the Maine Mall, not to shop, but to ride the escalator. We thought it was the coolest thing. He would hold our hands and we'd ride together, hundreds of times probably. "Again, Birdie!" we would say, and he wouldn't get impatient like most parents. He'd just laugh and say okay.

Tonight, I ride by myself. It's ten o'clock on a Friday in Boston, and I'm a teenager out on the town. I can eat what I want, buy what I want, go where I want — no parents anywhere. Woohoo!

At first there's a little thrill in it, but then it's gone. All I'm left with is the sick feeling in my stomach.

I walk over to a bench and sit down. My feet are tired from walking. My eyes are tired, too. I think about curling up right here and going to sleep. I could stay here all night. I could *live* here. Hey, those kids in *From the Mixed-up Files of Mrs. Basil E. Frankweiler* did it; they lived in the Met. Why not a train station? People are doing it right now. See? There's a homeless guy over there, using newspapers for a blanket.

Oh my God, there's a homeless guy over there, using news-papers for a blanket!

I am alone in a train station at ten-thirty at night, in a strange city. All I have left in my pocket is thirty-seven cents. And I am just moments away from getting strangled and thrown in a Dumpster.

I. Am freaking. Out.

I move to a different bench, closer to the security guard, but that doesn't make me feel any better. So I close my eyes.

Stella? It's me, Evyn.

Stell . . . ?

Are you there?

Nothing.

Please?

After all this time, the moment I need her most, she's gone. She's really gone. And I know this sounds crazy, but I miss her. I miss my dead mom that I never got the chance to know. I miss our talks, even if they weren't real. I miss her smile. I miss the way she could find good in any situation. I miss —

"Evyn?"

My eyes fly open.

Plaid shirt.

Stubble chin.

White, white teeth. Oh.

My. God.

Next to me there's an empty spot, and Linus sits down. He holds out a roll of mints, and I shake my head.

"We didn't know which train station," he says, peeling off a mint and popping it into his mouth. "So we had to split up."

I am too stunned to respond. I am too busy being glad I'm not wearing horse pajamas.

"Your friend called. Jules, is it? She was worried about you. So your dad took Back Bay, Thalia took 128th Street, and I came here."

You came here.

I can't think about Jules or my dad or anything. All I can think about is Linus's hand, which has found its way to my knee.

"Let me call home real quick."

He takes a phone out of his pocket and starts punching in numbers.

"Ma," he says, "I found her. South Station. Yeah, I think so." He turns to me. "You okay?"

I nod. *I am now.*

"She's fine. . . . Uh-huh. You want me to bring her back?"

And I don't know where I find the courage, but I grab his arm. When he looks at me, I shake my head like crazy.

"On second thought, Ma . . ."

And suddenly, miraculously, he starts wrangling with his mother about where I should spend the night. He uses terms like "decompression time" and "adolescent anxiety overload," and he is so incredible that he actually wins the argument.

I can't believe I am walking into a college dorm right now. No, not I. We. *We* are walking. Linus and me. Together.

"The room's a sty," he says. "Just to warn you."

"That's okay," I say. Because it is. Everything about Linus is okay. Better than okay. Everything about him is just right.

At this very moment, he is taking a keycard out of his pocket and sliding it into the door. I am about to walk into his dorm room, and I feel nervous and excited and, more than anything, ready for what will come next.

The door opens, and we walk through together. Me and Linus.

"Babe?"

Babe?

"Babe? Is that you?"

Me, Linus, and the most beautiful girl I have ever seen. No, not girl — definitely not girl — *woman.* Woman, jumping into his arms.

"Babe!"

I am speechless.

She has her legs wrapped around his waist, and he is rubbing her back, which is mostly skin because she's wearing some sort of skimpy number that barely covers anything. And when he puts her down, even though I don't want to, there is only one place to look and that's her chest.

"Evyn, this is my good friend Pamela."

Good friend. Right.

And after I have recovered from the size of her boobs, I look into her eyes and see that they are a color not found in nature. Not blue, not green, but something in between. Teal, maybe. With the longest lashes ever.

"Pamela, this is my sister Evyn."

"Hi, Evyn," she says. And of course there are the lips, and just when I am wondering if I could possibly be any more devastated, she says, "You're adorable!"

And she pats my head.

From my sleeping bag on the floor, I can hear them whispering.

Linus says, "She's having a tough time. I feel bad."

And Pamela says, "Yeah, I remember thirteen. It was awful. I was a band geek."

"C'mere, my little band geek," he says.

They kiss in the neon glow of the Budweiser sign on the wall. Both of their faces turning blue, then red, then blue again.

When I wake up, Pamela is gone.

The room smells like cigarettes. There's an empty wine bottle by the window, a glass with lipstick smudges all over it.

Linus is sitting on the couch, typing away on a laptop.

I watch him for a while. The curls. The shoulders. Everything.

When he looks up, he sees me and grins.

Oh, the dream teeth.

"Morning, kiddo."

And there you have it. *Kiddo*. Open heart, insert dagger.

"Your dad called," he says. "I told him I'd have you home by nine. I'll ride the T back with you."

When I don't respond he says, "Hey. Sorry about your dog. That sucks. Then the baby and everything. Double whammy."

I nod. I'm not sure I trust my voice right now.

"I'm sorry this is all happening to you."

His eyes are so beautiful I have to look away.

"If you ever want to talk about it . . ."

I stare at the floor.

"I mean it. Clio and Cassi call me all the time. You can, too."

"Really?"

He nods. "That's what family's for." And when he gets off the couch to hug me, it feels so warm and safe I want to stay here forever.

"Thanks," I say.

"You're welcome, kiddo," he says.

Kiddo. Again. Only this time, the dagger through my heart feels more like a butter knife.

Walking to the T, he asks if I care what sex the baby is.

"Not really," I say.

"You're not hoping for a girl?"

"Are you kidding? I have enough sisters already."

Then I realize what I said. I just called them my sisters. I am completely losing my mind.

CHAPTER TWENTY

Birdie won't let go. The minute I walked through the door, he grabbed me and started hugging, and now I can't move.

"You're cutting off my circulation," I say.

But he just squeezes harder. "Don't do that again."

"What?"

"Run off like that. You scared me."

"I wasn't even gone a whole day," I say.

"You *scared* me."

His voice is serious, and his voice is never serious, so I know he means it.

I tell him I won't do it again.

"Okay," he says.

He finally lets go, and we just stand there, neither of us talking. The silence makes my skin itch. I can't stand it.

"Hey. My sister the runaway."

Here is Mackey, holding a sandwich. Peanut butter, I can smell it. There are little orange gobs in the corners of his mouth.

"I didn't run away," I say. "I was just at the train station. *Thinking* about running away."

"Mmf."

Birdie says, "The important thing is she's home now."

My brother, overwhelmed with concern for his little sister, grunts and takes another bite.

Well, here we are, the three of us, standing in the front hall. Me, Mackey, and Birdie. The Linneys.

"So," I say, "*Al.* Where's your family?"

He says they're out.

"All of them?"

"Yup. It's just us chickens."

"Wow. *Al.* I can't believe they left you alone with us."

He tells me to give the Al thing a rest; he's still Birdie. "No matter what anyone calls me, I'm still your dad. I haven't changed."

I try not to roll my eyes, but my mouth has a mind of its own. "You can't be serious."

"What?" Birdie says.

"Everything *about* you has changed. You're a different person. You have contacts now. You wear *Weejuns.*"

Birdie looks confused. "Weejuns?"

"Your shoes," I say. "They're name-brand."

"Oh." He shrugs. "I don't know. Eleni bought them for me. They're remarkably comfortable. Here." He slips off a loafer. "Try one."

I ignore this and go on to talk about his lack of a beard, and his newfound love of spanakopita. "And since when do you like *golf*? Yesterday you were wearing a P.G.A. shirt."

To Mackey I say, "Right?"

He shrugs. "I didn't notice."

Birdie just looks bewildered. "A what shirt?"

Then I remember the four-course meal he cooked a few nights ago, and I get mad all over again. I say, "Imagine how you would feel, if I started doing things I'd never done before, with somebody else's dad."

I realize how stupid this sounds, but I keep going.

"And I made you go live at his house. And sleep in a room that smells like strawberry musk, with roommates who fight all the time. And eat hummus! And go to a school full of snotty girls in headbands!"

Mackey starts laughing, then choking on his sandwich.

I am torn between telling him to shut up and telling him to watch out, someone in this house knows the Heimlich.

"Ev," Birdie says. He leans in and kisses the top of my head. "Ev. Ev."

I try to duck away from him, but he won't let me. "C'mere," he says.

He scruffs his chin against my scalp, and I am quiet for a minute.

Then I say, "You never even asked us."

Birdie keeps on scruffing. "Hmm?"

"You just told us you were getting married. You didn't even ask first. You just went ahead and did it."

Mackey lets out a big peanut-butter burp.

"My feelings exactly," I say.

Birdie pulls back and looks at me. "We talked about it." Then, he looks at Mackey. "We *talked* about it. Remember the lobster?"

Mackey nods. "Good stuff."

"Yeah," I say. "That's when you *told* us you were getting married. You didn't *ask*. You told."

Birdie looks confused, which is confusing in itself. "I thought you liked Eleni. On Visiting Day you said she was great."

I did?

"That's not the point," I say.

Birdie shakes his head. "I said if you weren't okay with it, you should . . ." He hesitates. "Neither of you said anything. I thought . . ."

"You thought what?" I say. "You thought we were happy about it?"

"I thought I was doing something good. For all of us."

I stare at him.

"I finally met someone . . . I finally met someone I knew would be a good mother. And a good partner."

I look at Mackey, but he's looking at the floor, kicking at something with his toe.

"It took me . . ." Birdie stops to clear his throat. "It took me a long time to find Eleni."

What, was she lost in the woods, living in a hut made from birch bark, surviving on nothing but mushrooms and berries? The question is on my tongue, but I make myself swallow it. Now is not the time for humor.

Birdie takes a breath. "It took me a long time to fall in love again. I guess I just wanted our life together to start right away."

"Oh," I say. "Uh-huh."

"Because life is too short."

He keeps on going, but I am still recovering from the triple punch to my stomach. *Fall-uh! In-uh! Love-uh!*

"You never know when something is going to happen that will alter its course irreparably."

I look at Mackey, but he is still toeing the floor.

"It's not that I wasn't thinking about how you two would be affected," Birdie continues. "I was."

He looks from me to Mackey and back again. "I'm sorry," he says. His voice is low. "I'm sorry I didn't consult you first. You kids are the most important people in my life."

It kills me to ask it, but I have to. "More important than the *baby*?"

"Yes," Birdie says. He doesn't even hesitate. "More important than the baby."

Mackey looks up, finally. His face says he's as surprised as me.

"Why?" I ask, for both of us.

"Because," Birdie says, "I loved you first."

Upstairs, alone in my room, I can't stop thinking about what Birdie said. I lie on my storage-drawer bed, staring up at the lofts he built for the sweater twins. It's quiet in here for the first time in history, and the quiet is peaceful. A person could actually relax for once. But it's weird, too.

Stella?

Nothing.

I pick up a book and try to read, but that doesn't work, so I borrow some red nail polish and start painting my toes, which I have never done before, and it is a very messy and mildly distracting task, and then it's over. Only one thing left to do now, and that is analyze some more.

Because I loved you first.

There are so many ways he could have meant that. Maybe he was just trying to make me and Mackey feel better about the baby, but I don't think so. I think he was saying something more. More about our mom and how much he loved her. More about where Eleni fits into the whole picture. It's all so mixed up and complicated, and part of me does feel better, but another part feels worse. And I have no idea how to sort through it all.

In loving memory of Clam Moon-Muffin Linney.

This is what it says, on the front of the folded piece of paper someone just shoved under my door.

Then, on the inside:

Dear friends,
Please join us for an evening of solemn reflection
and heartfelt tributes
to Clam M. Linney,
the dog we loved so well.
Also, refreshments.

"What the hell is this?" I say to Birdie, waving the paper in his face. It took me a while to find him. He was smart to hide. But not smart enough to shut the pantry door.

"Are you responsible for this?" I say. "How did they know about Moon-Muffin?"

(I was four when we got Clam. Birdie let Mackey pick the first name, and I got to pick the middle name. I was *four*.)

Birdie turns to me, his hand in a box of crackers. "Hey, Ev." Crumbs spray everywhere. "You got the invitation? Good."

"Not good," I say. "They're not having a funeral for *our* dog. Anyway, you don't send invitations to funerals."

He puts the box on the shelf, then turns to me.

This wasn't his idea, he says. It was Phoebe's. Apparently, she organized the whole thing, it starts at six, and all I need to do is show up.

"Phoebe didn't even *know* Clam," I say. "None of them did. I mean, come on. Eleni made him sleep in the yard, which is probably why he died anyway. From neglect."

"Thalia's allergic to pet dander," he says. "And I doubt neglect had anything to do with it. Clam was old. In dog years, he was sixty-three."

When I don't respond, Birdie tells me to be gracious. Everyone has been working hard to give Clam a nice send-off.

"That's what they're out doing?" I say. "Planning a funeral for a dog they hardly knew?"

"Yup."

He reaches into his pocket. It's toothpick time.

"Are you kidding me?" I say.

"Nope."

"*God.*"

I stare at my father, while he finishes removing every last molecule of food from his teeth.

"Anyway," he says, turning to me, "what makes you think they're doing this for Clam?"

The funeral is held in the backyard. You can barely recognize the place. There are origami birds perched on every surface, and where there aren't birds there are strands of Christmas lights, and where there aren't Christmas lights there are miniature dog bones and Beggin' Strips hanging from fishing line.

It is a scene so ridiculous that my first instinct is to crack up. But then Phoebe appears, and she's wearing a black floppy hat with a veil, and her orange Gartos-Linney Utopian Experiment T-shirt, and that urge is squashed flat. There is nothing funny about her outfit.

Phoebe hands me yet another folded piece of paper. On the front is a brown crayon dog — or what I assume was meant to be a dog but looks more like a bear with balloon hands. She leads me to a semicircle of lawn chairs in the middle of the yard and gestures to one with a big yellow stain on it — maybe lemonade, maybe pee.

I sit.

"I'm sorry for your loss."

She's whispering, even though we're the only ones here.

Now she's patting my arm. "Clam is in a better place. They never run out of bones there, you know."

I don't want to smile, I really don't. But I can't help it. I hold up the program and say, "Did you draw this?"

"Uh-huh."

"Nice."

Phoebe hands me a pack of mini tissues and takes off.

I wait.

After a while, music starts playing. A voice yells, "Is that loud enough?"

I look up and there's Cleanser Boy, leaning out the third-floor window, holding a speaker. I yell back, "Yeah!"

"Sorry in advance for the music selection! Phoebe's orders!"

I close my eyes and listen — and it's surprisingly uplifting, actually, to have a bunch of orphans tell me how hard-knock their life is.

Finally, everyone starts filing out of the house. They are lined up smallest to tallest — Von Trapp style — which might be cute, if they were wearing the matching window-drape outfits, but no. It's the matching GLUE shirts.

Once again, I am dressed wrong, but that doesn't explain the feeling in my stomach. The mad-sad-could-barf-any-second-now combo. I know my face is turning red, but it's not the crush-blush. It has nothing to do with Linus, even though here he is, in line with the rest of them, smiling at me.

I smile back, barely.

The last one out of the house is Mackey because he's tallest, and on top of the GLUE shirt he's wearing . . . what the hell is he wearing? Some sort of a fluorescent patchwork-quilt cape, tied around his neck in a big bow, with fringe hanging off it and —

Ah.

The Dreamcoat.

Of course.

Because we wouldn't want this dog funeral to be missing anything obvious.

Birdie takes the seat next to me. "Hi, Ev," he whispers.

I whisper, "Are you kidding me with this?"

Now Phoebe is standing in the middle of the semicircle, her hand raised for silence.

Everyone gets quiet, but Annie keeps right on singing. Her voice is clear, her outlook sunny. She thinks she's gonna like it here.

No, Annie! Run! Back to the orphanage! You're not gonna like it here, trust me! They're freak shows!

Then someone cuts the music, and Phoebe peers out at us from under her veil. "Dearly beloved," she begins. The way six-year-old funeral directors always do.

She says things about Clam that could fit any dog. What nice soft ears he had, and how he always gave her hand a big lick when she came outside. Then she tells us that her whole life she'd been asking, "Can we *please* get a dog?" And the answer was always "No, we can get a goldfish." But the goldfish were constantly jumping out of the bowl or eating each other.

"Finally," Phoebe says, "the Linneys came, and my dog wish finally, finally, finally came true! Finally!" She pauses. "Even though he died, too." Another pause. "May he rest in peace."

Then she bows and everyone claps, which doesn't seem like normal funeral behavior to me. But then, there is nothing normal about these people.

"Bravo!" Birdie yells out. "Bravissimo!"

Next up, Thalia.

In her flowy skirt, with her flowy hair, bare feet, and still the single eyebrow, she reads a poem that sounds like it came straight from English class. According to my program it is "The Road Less Traveled" by Robert Frost. The whole time she's reading about roads and woods and traveling, I am thinking, *What does this have to do with anything?* Anyone who knew Clam can tell you he was not much for the woods. He was an ocean dog.

Also according to my program, Cleanser Boy is in charge of lighting and sound, the sweater twins are the decorations committee, Betty Boop cooked (of course), and Birdie made the casket for the deceased.

I look around. *Casket? What casket?*

"Clam," Thalia says to the air, "wherever you are, whatever road you have taken, may it always be paved with dog biscuits."

Has anything more ridiculous ever been said? No, it has not.

And yet, here comes the applause again.

Birdie leans over and whispers, "How're you holding up?"

I'm about to say something sarcastic, but now Phoebe is grabbing his hand. "Al. Come on. You need to dig the hole."

"I need to dig the hole," he tells me, getting up.

Fine. Whatever. Go dig your hole.

This is Eleni's cue to slide into my father's seat and pretend to be my mother. She pats my knee. She pats, she pats, while I grit my teeth, grit my teeth. Finally, she stands up and you can see that she is bigger already. The fabric of her GLUE shirt is stretched tight across her middle.

"I know this isn't on the program," she says, "but I'd like to read something."

I can't stop staring at her stomach.

"I wasn't going to do this," she says.

I think, *So why are you?*

"This isn't easy for me because . . ." Big throat clear. "Well, I haven't read this poem in almost thirty years."

Yikes. You are wayyy too old to be having a baby.

This is what I'm thinking when she says what she says next.

"The last time I read it was at my mother's funeral."

The words fly around in my head, even though I don't want them to. *At my mother's funeral. At my mother's funeral.*

I feel my stomach flip over. I don't want to think about mothers right now. This is not about mothers; this is about dogs. This is about Clam.

I look around for Birdie and spot him in the corner of the yard, holding a shovel. He's not digging, though, he's leaning on it. His eyes are right on Eleni.

"'Remember.' By Christina Georgina Rossetti."

The yard is completely silent, except for her. She doesn't look at any paper. She has the whole thing memorized.

"Remember me," she says, looking around at everyone.

I stare at the grass and think, *Shut up.*

"When I am gone away."

Shut. Up.

"When you can no more hold me by the hand, Nor I half turn to go, yet turning stay."

Shutupshutupshutupshutup.

144

Her voice gets lower and lower, but she keeps going. And by the time she gets to telling us we should "forget and smile" instead of "remember and be sad," something has taken over my good sense and I am crying. Not quiet, pretty tears, either. The big, loud, ugly kind.

And no matter how hard I try, I can't stop. Not even when Linus comes over to hug me.

And when Birdie lowers the wooden box he made into the hole he dug, and they all toss dirt and origami birds and dog treats on top, and Mackey lays down a rock for a grave marker, I let everyone think I'm crying because of Clam.

It's two in the morning, and I can't sleep. I have to know. I have to talk to Birdie right now, but of course he's in bed with Eleni.

I stand outside their room, and I don't hear any disgusting noises, so I open the door.

"Birdie," I whisper.

But he's not the one who pops up. It's her, hair spiking every which way. "Evyn? Is that you?"

"Yeah."

At least she's wearing a nightgown.

"Are you okay?"

"I need to talk to my dad," I say.

She leans over and touches his shoulder. "Al? Sweetheart? Wake up. Evyn's here."

"Huhwhat? What? Huh?"

Birdie is still half asleep, but he rolls out of bed and scuffs along behind me into the peachy bathroom. He scuffs right over to the sink and grabs his toothbrush.

"Birdie."

"Hmm."

"What are you *doing*? It's the middle of the night. Who brushes their teeth in the middle of the night?"

He mumbles something about plaque buildup and turns on the water.

I watch him and watch him, and I feel myself get more and more mad. I don't plan to do it, but something takes over, and I rip the toothbrush out of his hand and throw it in the trash.

Then, I ask my question.

"Do you miss her?"

Birdie frowns into the trash can. There are pillow creases on his cheek. Did he even hear me? I'll promise you one thing, if he asks who, I will run out that door and never come back.

I watch as he opens his mouth. Shuts it. Opens it again.

"Just answer," I say. "It's not complicated. Do you? Do you miss her?"

Finally, he nods. "Every day."

I take a deep breath. "Do you still love her?"

Instead of responding, he slumps sideways against the peachy tile and closes his eyes.

At first I think he's fallen asleep, and I feel myself get mad, but then his eyes pop open, and there they are. Tears. Not pouring down his cheeks, but still. Real tears, shining there. He opens his mouth, but he can't say anything. And that, to me, says everything.

I put my hand on his arm. "Me, too. I know it sounds dumb, but it's true. I still miss her every day."

He shakes his head. "It doesn't sound dumb."

I think about Stella. I wonder what Birdie would think if I told him about our talks.

"Your mother was too good for this world," he says. "She could light up a room with her smile. She was —"

"I know!" I blurt out. Then, softer, "I *know*. My whole life you've been telling me how great she was. Too good for this world. Lighting up rooms left and right. Bouncing all over the place. And my whole life I've been trying to be like that, but I'm not. . . ." I pause, thinking about how to say it. "That's just not my . . . *modus operandi*. Okay?"

Birdie smiles. "Aren't you glad you stuck with Latin?"

I give him a look.

"Ev." Now his face is serious. "You don't have to be like her. All you have to be — all I ever want you to be — is *you*."

"Uh-huh."

His hand is on my hand. "Your mom was a wonderful person — an *extraordinary* person — but she wasn't perfect. She had flaws, just like the rest of us. There were things about her that drove me nuts."

"Really?"

He nods.

"Tell me," I say.

"Oh, I don't know. She would clip her toenails in the kitchen and then just leave the clippings on the floor. . . . And she was absentminded. Almost pathologically so. *Constantly* misplacing things. Keys. Wallets. Sunglasses. At least once a day, it was 'Honey, have you seen my sunglasses? Where did I put my sunglasses?' "

He leans back against the tile, closing his eyes, letting himself remember. "And she never thought she was dressed right. We'd be on our way out the door and she'd have to run back inside to change her clothes. It didn't matter how many times I told her she looked beautiful. She still had to change."

I do that, too. Only it's not just in my head, it's a fact: Ninety percent of the time I'm wearing the opposite of cool.

"The thing is," Birdie says, "when you really love a person, you don't just embrace the good qualities. Those are easy. You have to embrace the flaws as well. That's the beauty of love. That's what makes it real."

"Toenail clippings?" I say.

He smiles. "Toenail clippings."

We're quiet for a minute. Then I look right at him. "I'm glad you still love Mom." It feels good to say it, a big relief.

Birdie nods slowly. "I will always love your mom. But . . ." He takes a deep breath, and I know exactly what's coming next. *She's gone, and she's not coming back, and Betty Boop is here to stay.*

"But you love Eleni," I say.

"Yes. I love Eleni. And I love her kids. But that doesn't mean I love you and Mackey any less. Can you understand that?"

I give him a tiny nod.

"I know this has been hard for you."

"It has been," I say, and my throat gets froggy. "Really hard."

"I know," he says, and I can tell from his voice that he means it.

Birdie hugs me, and I let him. I let him do the old chin scruff, the way he's always done, minus the beard.

"Thank you for continuing to try," he says.

I nod. I'm not exactly agreeing with him, but I'm not fighting it, either.

"Okay?" he asks.

"Yeah."

Maybe the next time we talk I'll tell him about the It Girls, and about Jules trading me in for Jessie Kapler, and how I'm afraid no boy will ever want to kiss me. But for now, I'm tired. It's funny how you can go from not being able to sleep at all to being so exhausted you can't even see straight.

CHAPTER TWENTY-ONE

On Monday morning, a small miracle happens. Mrs. Kilgallon changes the desks around. Now, instead of the Chelsea-Jaime death squeeze, I get an empty seat on my left and a girl with black China doll bangs on my right. The minute I sit down, she turns to me. "I'm Kate."

"I'm Evyn," I say.

"I know. You have math with C.B."

"C.B.?"

"Clara Bing. No one calls her Clara Bing."

Sneezy Dwarf, I think. Then I feel bad.

"Short?" Kate says. "Brown hair? Blowing her nose all the time? She's one of my best friends."

"The Four-Foot-Two Crew," I say.

"Right. She told us about you. We keep looking for you at lunch."

You do?

"But you're never there."

Right.

She eyes me suspiciously. "You *do* eat lunch, right? You're not one of those girls who's trying to starve herself down to a toothpick, are you?"

I shake my head. "No."

"Good. Because we like to eat."

"I have the most disgusting lunches in the world," I blurt out. "My stepmother's Greek, so . . ."

Kate shrugs. "Mine's macrobiotic. Wait until you taste her brewer's-yeast-and-wheat-germ quiche. Picture a pile of dog doo. Now add a crust of sweat."

She pantomimes barfing into her backpack.

I laugh.

I think it's the first time I've laughed in this school.

Latin class. Mr. Murray is so excited to act out *Julius Caesar* it's scary. I've decided he has no life outside of teaching. How else do you explain the toga-and-leaf-crown ensemble he sewed himself? I should introduce him to Thalia. I bet they'd really hit it off.

"The advantage of having a small class," Mr. Murray says, "is we get to play all the plum roles!"

Plum roles.

Plum.

And I'm Evyn Plum.

Argh.

Ever since my mortifying first encounter with Travis Piesch-not-Peach, I have not been able to relax around him. I don't know what it is. It's not like he's cute or anything. Well, maybe the glasses are. And the eyes, which I've noticed are greenish with gold flecks. But he says "*um*" every other word, which is annoying. And anyway, he takes Latin, so how cool could he be? He's no Linus, I can tell you that.

After Mr. Murray hands out the scripts, he has to run to his car for something. He doesn't leave the room like a normal teacher, though. He says, "O you hard hearts, you cruel men of Rome! I shall return anon!"

What are you supposed to say to that?

I think about getting up to go to the bathroom, but then Travis starts talking. He tells me he's read all of Shakespeare's tragedies.

I say I've read all of the Sweet Valley High series.

"Is that, um, chick lit?" he asks.

"I was kidding."

"Oh."

Now there's silence, and it's so awkward I start to get up again, but then he says something else. "I'm not a dork, if that's what you're thinking."

And it's my turn to say *um*.

He tells me his parents are Elizabethan scholars. Their idea of a good time is the whole family reading aloud from *The Riverside Shakespeare* over roast leg of lamb.

"Lamb?" I say.

He makes a face. "With mint sauce."

"You're kidding."

"Uh-uh."

"Believe it or not," I say, "I happen to have a lamb-and-mint-sauce sandwich in my bag right now. . . . I'm completely serious. You want proof?"

I start rustling through my backpack for the lunch Eleni packed. When I find it, I hold it up like a trophy. "Taa daa!"

Travis smiles, and for a second he looks the tiniest bit like Johnny Depp. Not that I'm a huge Johnny Depp fan or anything, but —

"*Salve,* countrymen!"

Mr. Murray comes charging through the door in his toga, arms full of props, and it's back to *Julius Caesar.*

Lunch.

I stand in the middle of the cafeteria, looking around. Then I feel a hand on my arm.

"Evyn?"

It's Clara Bing — correction, *C.B.* — standing there. Her nose is red and raw-looking, and there's crust in her eyelashes.

"You're sitting with us, right?" she says.

I nod.

"Come on," she says, and I follow her to a table by the windows. I look around and feel relief. There's a girl with short hair like mine, one with a red paisley do-rag and even a tongue ring. Nary a headband to be found.

Why didn't I notice these girls before?

"You know Kate, right?" C.B. says. "From homeroom? And this is Pia. And Grier. And Ally."

As C.B. makes the intros, everyone looks me in the eye and actually says my name. "Hi, Evyn."

And, unlike the It Girls, they do not spend the entire lunch period talking about boys and lip gloss. Mostly it is the books they've read, and movies they've seen, and books they've read that they think should be made into movies, and books they've read that have already been made into movies but shouldn't have.

They talk about Harry Potter. They talk about *The Penderwicks* and *The Catcher in the Rye*.

Mostly I just listen, but every so often one of them will stop and say, "What do you think, Evyn?"

And even though we just met, I want to hug them all. Because it has been so long since anyone asked me what I thought about anything.

When the bell rings, C.B. and I walk to math together. On our way through the hall, we have to pass Andrea and her underlings.

As we do, one of them shoots me a dirty look. Another one calls me the B-word, loud. Everyone is staring. I feel like I've been punched in the gut.

C.B. leans in. "Hey," she says softly. "You okay?"

I try to smile but don't quite make it.

Then, just as we're about to enter the math room, she sneezes about fifteen times in a row, and on the final one, a snot rocket shoots out her nose and lands on my elbow. It just hangs there, like a big yellow slug.

It's probably the most disgusting thing I've ever seen, but somehow, miraculously, I am cracking up. So is C.B. We're both laughing so hard the math teacher won't let us come in until we've calmed down.

Eleni is in the kitchen when I get home, and she does the same thing she always does when she sees me: smiles like crazy, asks how I am, and tries to make me eat something she made.

"How's school going?" she asks.

I shrug.

"Are you enjoying your classes? Your teachers? Meeting some nice girls?"

She really has no idea how to get me to talk. Adults who ask questions like that don't have a clue about teenagers. Why do they even bother?

But I remember what Birdie said last night, about me continuing to try. So I answer her questions.

They're okay.

They're okay.

Yeah. A few.

"Well," she says now, arranging pita wedges into the shape of a fan, "I'm really looking forward to the Mother-Daughter Tea. The first time I went, when Thalia was in eighth grade . . ."

She keeps talking, but I've stopped listening. My head is saying *Mother-Daughter Tea? Whaaaat?* I picture Eleni going through the trash. Hunched over the kitchen table, taping scraps of the invitation back together.

"Since I'm on the baking committee, I thought I'd pick your brain about desserts. Any ideas?"

Um.

Then she says, "I would have asked you sooner, but I haven't felt like being in the same *room* with food for a while, let alone cooking anything. But now that I'm over the hump, so to speak . . ."

She pats her belly, and all I can think is, *A while? How long is "a while"?*

Now she is smiling, eager, and I know I can do one of two things: run out of the room screaming, or continue to try, for Birdie's sake.

So I say, "Chocolate."

"Chocolate," she repeats.

"Yeah. Everyone loves chocolate. Even snobs."

CHAPTER TWENTY-TWO

Friendship is a funny thing.

Just when I'm convinced I will never make a friend in the city of Boston, the Four-Foot-Two Crew adopts me — or at least they've asked me to sit at their lunch table every day since Monday.

And just when I think Jules has forgotten me forever, she calls.

"Who?" I say, when Birdie hands me the phone. "Jules *who*? I used to know a Jules, but that was years ago."

In my coolest voice, I say, "I assume you called to apologize."

But what I get is not an apology. What I get is classic Jules.

"Jordan Meyerhoff is a *bleepity-bleeping-bleep-bleeper.* I don't care if I never see his *bleeping* face again in my life, that *bleeper!*"

"Tell me how you really feel," I say.

"Jessie Kapler can kiss my *bleeping bleep.* I can't believe I ever trusted her. The minute I turn around, she stabs me in the *bleeping* back? That two-faced *bleep!*"

Well. This would be a prime opportunity to say, "I told you so," or to slam down the phone, just to teach her a lesson. But as soon as she's finished swearing, she starts crying. And there's nothing worse than listening to your best friend blow snot bubbles into the phone.

"Jules," I say. "Jules, hey. It's okay."

"No," she says. "It is not *okay.* My so-called *boyfriend* hooked up with my so-called *friend.* That is what I would call the opposite of *okay.*"

I bite my tongue. What I have to do in this situation is to let her keep going as long as she needs to — until she gets it all out of her system. Because that is what a best friend does.

Then, when there's a lull, I open my mouth. "She's pregnant, you know."

This stops Jules dead in her tracks.

"*What?*" she says. "Jessie's *pregnant?*"

"Not Jessie. Birdie's wife. Eleni."

"Ohhhh," she says. "Betty Boop."

"Right." I'd forgotten I'd told her the name.

"Betty Boop and Birdie are having a baby?"

"Yeah."

Jules snorts. "That sounds so funny. *Betty Boop and Birdie are having a baby.* Say it ten times fast. *BettyBoop andBirdieare —*"

"Jules."

"What?"

"Knock it off."

"Sorry," she says.

"It's okay."

"It's just, how did this happen? I mean, I know how it *happened,* but, how is this even possible? How old is she?"

"Old."

"What does Mackey think?"

"Who knows?" I say.

Then I tell her I'm pretty sure Eleni was pregnant at the wedding.

"Ooooo," Jules says. "Sex before marriage. Blasphemy."

"It's not that," I say. "It's just . . ."

"What."

"I don't know. I don't know if she *knew* she was pregnant before and didn't tell Birdie, or if they *both* knew and just didn't tell us, and if they both knew, is that why he asked her to marry him? Is that why we moved so fast? And if that's the only reason he asked her, then does he even really love her? And if he doesn't really love her . . . well . . ."

"Whoa," Jules says.

"I know."

Then I say I don't want to talk about it anymore. I just want to change the subject.

"Okay." Jules perks up. "So. Have you met anyone as cool and beautiful and funny as me yet?"

"Not yet," I say. Which is true.

But I tell her about the Four-Foot-Two Crew — how they may not be the most popular girls in school, but they aren't boring, either. Today at lunch, they taught me their theory of dork-twins and cool-twins.

"It's like this," I say. "A dork-twin is an uglier version of yourself, and a cool-twin is a hotter version of yourself, and they can both be mistaken for you from a distance."

"Like a doppelgänger."

"Exactly. And by that same logic, you are also someone *else's* dork-twin and someone *else's* cool-twin."

"Example," Jules says.

"Okay. Take your mom's secretary friend. The blond one. Really, really skinny."

"Winnie," Jules says. "Skinny Winnie."

"Right."

"What about her?"

"Cameron Diaz's dork-twin."

And Jules says, "Oh, *yeah*. I totally see that!"

"I know, right? But don't feel bad because she has her *own* dork-twin, too. Who knows where she lives in the world. Maybe Paris."

"Ah," Jules says. "This goes international."

"Apparently. My friend Kate? She was in Amsterdam once, and she saw her cousin Ralphie's dork-twin, right outside Anne Frank's house. He was Ralphie to a tee, except with stringier hair and a hunchback. And he was picking his nose."

"Huh," Jules says.

"You can cross genders, too. Ally has a cool-twin at Thorne. His name's Peter, but to us he's *Mally,* for *Male Ally.* He's one of those longhair hotties. Ally says he's even prettier than she is, but she's not offended or anything. It's just a fact. And then, there's this guy in my Latin class? Travis? And I think he might be Johnny Depp's dork-twin. Only he's kind of cute. Not that I like him or anything, but . . ."

I stop, realizing that Jules hasn't said anything for a while. "Hey," I say. "Are you still there?"

"Uh-huh."

"I know it sounds dumb, but once you start thinking about it, you become *obsessed* with it. I mean, *everyone* has a dork-twin, and *everyone* has a cool-twin. Think about it. It's like this gigantic, unifying —"

"Ev."

"Yeah."

"It's not that," she says. "It's just . . . I don't know."

"What."

"I don't know. It just sounds like you're having a really good time. With your new friends and everything. I think I might be jealous."

"*What?* I'm not having a good time. I hate it here."

"Ev."

"I *do*. I hate it. I want to be back in Maine."

I let myself go on about Eleni and the baby and the sweater twins and my lack of chest and the It Girls, until Jules cuts me off.

"You're kidding, right?" she says.

"No."

"Huh."

"What."

She's quiet for a second. Then she says, "You don't sound like you."

"What do you mean I don't sound like me? This *is* me."

"No. Usually you're so, I don't know, *glass is half full* about everything. You're always the one who can cheer me up, put things in perspective —"

"*What?*" I say. "No, I'm not."

"Yes, you are."

"I am very negative."

Jules laughs. "Please."

I say, "No. I am. You should be inside my head. You should hear the things I think all day. It's like . . . I don't know. I just wish I could be different sometimes. I wish I could be better."

It feels weird saying this out loud, but it's a good weird.

"Who doesn't want to be better?" Jules says. "Come on, Ev. Give yourself a break."

She goes on to remind me of some of the highlights of our friendship: the time her cat, Mr. Pickles, got trapped behind the fridge (I gave him mouth-to-mouth); the time Randy Garvin called her a slut (I kneed him in the nuts); the day Agnes left for college and Jules couldn't stop crying (I made her a tear-bottle necklace).

"I'm sorry," Jules says. "About everything. You're the best person I know."

"Well," I say. "I'm no Jessie Kapler. . . ."

"Don't even mention that *bleeper*'s name! I hate that *bleeping bleep*!"

I think, *Here we go again.* But I realize there's nowhere I'd rather be right now than on the phone with my best friend, listening to her hailstorm of profanity.

CHAPTER TWENTY-THREE

Mother-Daughter Tea day.

I wake up with dread in my stomach. Lying in bed, I wonder how I could get out of this. Fake period cramps? Hold a thermometer up to the light until it reaches 103 (a trick Jules swears by but I have never tried)? Break my own arm?

"Where's my Red Hot Mama nail polish? Did you take my Red Hot Mama nail polish?"

Eight-fifteen on a Sunday morning, and the sweater twins are at it already.

"I didn't take your stupid nail polish," the other one says. "I don't even *wear* nail polish."

"Shut up, Clio. You do too. You wore it to the wedding."

"Yeah. That was for a special occasion. Anyway, it was pink. Pink is classy. Red is for —"

"You'd better not be calling me a —"

"Be quiet!" I yell.

They both turn to me, dumbfounded.

I am a little dumbfounded myself. I didn't plan to do it; it just slipped out. I take a breath and say, "Will you please just stop? I took it, okay? I took your stupid nail polish, and I'm sorry. Here." I reach over to the bedside table and grab the bottle. "Take it."

She does, without a word.

Somehow I find the courage to keep going. "Why do you two fight all the time? I mean, if you hate each other so much, why don't you just switch rooms with Thalia or something?"

They look at me, surprised.

"We don't hate each other," says the first one.

And the other one says, "We're sisters. Sisters fight."

"But we're still best friends. We'd still give each other an organ if necessary. Or bone marrow. Right, Cass? You'd have spinal fluid drained for me."

"Absolutely."

I shrug. "Whatever you say."

They go on to tell me how it's not the same with brothers. The girls in this family don't fight with Linus and Ajax like they do with each other. It's a different bond entirely. More intimate, more intense.

"Like with us and Mom, when she's being a total wench. Right, Clio?"

"Right. Mothers are like sisters to the ninth degree."

I say, "I guess I wouldn't know."

The sweater twins look at me, curious, and then it kicks in. Here come the apologies.

"It's okay," I tell them. "I'm used to it. Like today, this Mother-Daughter Tea thing. I'll be the only one there without a mom. I mean, it's nice of Eleni to come with me and everything, but it's not . . . you know. It's not the same."

They both look at me, quiet for once.

One of them comes over and sits next to me. "I'm sorry," she says. "That must be really hard."

"I'm sorry, too," says the other one. Then, "*God.* The Mother-Daughter Tea. Remember that dress you wore? That doily thing?"

"Oh my God. With the lace shoes."

It's amazing how quickly they go back to being themselves.

"So, what are you wearing, Evyn?"

"I have something you can wear."

"*Not* the doily."

"Shut up, Cassi. I wouldn't do that to her. I have the perfect Mother-Daughter Tea outfit."

"Sure you do."

I listen to them go back and forth for a while, arguing about what would be my best look. Then I cut them off.

"Stop!" I say.

They stop.

"You two are *not* dressing me! I mean, I appreciate the offer and everything, but I think it's time I dressed myself."

Here is what I have on: my favorite corduroys, worn thin at the knees, and plain white sneakers with Ped socks. On top is the sweater Jules gave me for my eleventh birthday — frayed collar, holey elbows. When I get to the kitchen I look straight at Eleni and say, "This is what I'm wearing."

She has on a blue dress with a flower pattern, heels, little pearl studs. The ultimate tea-drinking outfit.

I wait for her to tell me, *No way, go change, that's inappropriate.*

But she doesn't. She nods and says, "You look comfortable."

Yes. That is exactly what I am. Comfortable. For the first time in a long time, I am dressed like me. Evyn Linney: Ace Slob.

"Girl after my own heart," Birdie says, an expression that has never made sense to anyone.

He's busy wrapping foil over a platter of baked goods — brownies, blondies, cookies, and some unidentifiable chocolate object on a stick.

"You know," Eleni says, "I think I'll wear slacks, too."

I don't know what bothers me more — the word *slacks* or the fact that she's going to change her clothes.

As soon as she leaves the room, I say, "Great. Now we can be twins."

Birdie pretends not to hear.

I try again. "Why do old people always say *slacks* instead of *pants*?"

"Forty-something isn't old," he says. "*Forty* is —"

"Please don't say *Forty is the new thirty.* Everything is always 'the new something.' *Big is the new small. Red is the new black.* It's annoying."

Birdie smiles, holds up a chocolate stick thing. "Fudge is the new fruit?"

"Al is the new Birdie?"

"Ha-ha."

At the March School, we follow the pink, scalloped MOTHER-DAUGHTER TEA signs to the cafeteria and look around for the dessert section. Eleni spots it, then goes to deliver her platter o' chocolate.

The room has been transformed. Instead of the usual beige, it is a vision in pink — pink tablecloths, pink napkins, pink teacups, pink chairs. Which I guess is better than yellow-and-green plaid, but still. It looks like a Pepto-Bismol convention.

All the tables have been named after flowers. We locate our little pink card. MISS EVYN LINNEY AND MRS. ELENI LINNEY: NASTURTIUM. I notice that Clara Bing and Joyce Bing are tulips. Bummer.

On our way through the room, Eleni warms up her small-talk muscles. Did I know nasturtium is edible?

No, I did not.

It's true, by golly! Flower blossoms can be chopped up to flavor butter, sour cream, or vinegar, and whole flowers can be a colorful and delicious accent to salads or even a garnish!

"You seem to really like cooking," I say.

She nods vigorously. Then she tells me she'd be happy to collaborate on a meal, anytime. Maybe a night this week. What's my favorite food?

I look at her. "Gum."

"Gum?" she says. "I know a great recipe." She winks. "It dates back to my great- great-great-Greek-grandmother. Tastes like chicken."

This is the kind of joke Birdie would make — so corny it almost hurts.

"There it is," she says, pointing. "Nasturtium."

I look over. Three mothers in flower-print dresses and pearls, three daughters to match.

Seeing them together, my stomach hurts. It's the same feeling I get every year around Mother's Day. While every other kid in class is busy writing the "I Love My Mom" poem and making the requisite clay pot in art, I get pulled aside by some nice teacher who asks if there's another special person I'd like to make something for. An aunt? A neighbor?

"Evyn?" Eleni is looking at me now. "You okay?"

"Dandy," I say.

We sit. I focus on faces.

Girl from my English class.

Girl from my history class.

Andrea.

Crap. CRAP.

We do the intros.

Grace. Her mom, Katherine. Liza. Her mom, Judy.

Eleni says, "Hi. We're Eleni and Evyn," which makes us sound like business partners. Hi, we're Abercrombie & Fitch. But at least she sidesteps the stepmother thing.

The woman next to me introduces herself as Diane. She has the same sun-streaked hair as Andrea, the same wide gray eyes. But when she dangles her long pink fingers in front of me, I grasp them and think, *Cold fish.*

Andrea hasn't looked at me yet. Her eyes are fixed on the sugar bowl, like she's waiting for something to pop out. Diane hisses, "Stop slumping."

For a minute I think I must have imagined it. Andrea is upright. Diane is flashing her pretty teeth across the table. "Judy, I met your husband. Hugh, is it? At the club the other night. He told me about your trip to Japan. . . ."

The small talk revs up. International travel. Drapes. Predictions for another cold winter. Grace asks me about the history assignment. Eleni shares her recipe for lamb curry.

But then I hear it again. "Get your hair out of your face. Right now. You look like a slob."

Diane turns to Eleni. "So. What does *your* husband do?"

I watch out of the corner of my eye as Andrea takes off her headband. She smooths back her shiny blond hair again and again.

The head of the school does her big welcome. Committee moms get up and thank other committee moms. There's a lot of air kissing.

Finally, it's time to eat.

I stand behind Andrea and her mother in the buffet line and try to tune out, but it's impossible. "Put that *back*. Do you know how many fat grams are in a cruller?" Diane's plate has half a grapefruit, three blueberries, and a wedge of lemon. Andrea reaches toward the fruit. "Not with your *fingers*. The *tongs*." Andrea nods and picks up the tongs as though they're made of glass. When she tries to transfer a blueberry to her plate, it rolls off the table onto the floor. Diane snorts. "You're so graceful." Then, "Hurry *up*. People are waiting. What, do you think you're *better* than everyone?"

I feel sick.

I put a scone on my plate, but I know I'm not going to eat it. I just need to be holding something.

Maybe this isn't what it seems. Maybe Andrea's mom is having one of those days; she's on her period, or someone in the family is sick. No one's getting enough sleep, everyone's irritable.

I imagine a scene with them in the car later, Diane's hand on Andrea's arm. "I'm sorry I snapped at you in there, honey. I don't know what came over me. I love you." A hug. Something. Anything. But deep inside, I can't make myself believe it.

In the parking lot, Eleni rests her head against the steering wheel. "That was awful."

I tell her I know. I've never seen anything like it in my life.

"I should have said something. Should I have said something?"

I shrug. "What are you supposed to say? She's the mother."

"Exactly. She's the mother. She's the *mother*."

I watch as she puts on her seat belt. She tries to slide the keys into the ignition but can't quite do it. Her hands are shaking. I hope this doesn't mean we're going to crash.

I decide to change the subject. Fast.

"Your desserts were a big hit. Especially those stick things. What were those?"

"The chocolate bomba pops?"

"Chocolate bomba pops. Yes. Those looked great."

She turns to me. "You didn't get one?"

"I wish," I say. I tell her I sort of lost my appetite, what with all the barbs and the insults and fat grams flying around. "Now I'm hungry."

"Me, too," she says. "Starving." She asks if I want to go grab something to eat.

I nod.

"Good," she says. "I'll take you to my dirty little secret."

We're in line at the Burger Basket — BEST BURGERS IN BEAN-TOWN. I've heard about this place. It's one of the premier grease pits in the city, second only to Kelly's Roast Beef.

The air smells like lard. My stomach does a little jig of excitement.

"I can't believe you eat here," I say.

"I don't." Eleni squints at the menu. "The baby does."

Please, I think. *Please don't ruin this for me. I want french fries too badly.*

"With Linus and Ajax, it was ice cream. With the girls, it was always grease and salt." She pats her stomach. "This one's a girl. I know it."

I wonder how she feels about that — another daughter. Isn't she sick of daughters?

Our food comes. We take it to a booth in the corner. Grease streaks on the table, shriveled-up straw wrappers and dribbles of milk shake. Finally, my outfit matches my environment.

I stuff four fries in my mouth at once, Mackey-style.

Eleni takes a bite of burger. Then another. And another. Finally, she puts it down. "That poor girl."

"Who? Andrea?"

"I can't stop thinking about it," she says. "That poor, poor girl." How anyone, how any *mother,* could talk that way to her daughter is incomprehensible. She can't imagine taking her children for granted like that. She can't imagine doing anything but loving them, being grateful for every second.

"Life is too short," she tells me. "Remember that."

"I know," I say.

She reaches for more fries and realizes she's out. She looks at my basket. "Do you mind?"

"Go ahead."

"Sorry," she says. "I can't seem to get enough grease."

"It's okay. I'm done."

"My mother died," she says, fiddling with the fries in front of her. "When I was twelve."

I think about Clam's funeral, the poem she hadn't read in almost thirty years. So — quick math — she's almost forty-two. Forty-two and pregnant with Birdie's baby. I wonder if she'll love it as much as the first six. I wonder if she'll love it more.

"My mom died, too," I blurt out. "When I was one."

"I know," she says.

Of course she does, because Birdie told her. He probably tells her everything.

"Do you have any memories of her?" Eleni asks.

I give her the look teenagers give stupid grown-ups. "I was *one.*"

She nods. "I know. People say you can't remember anything before age three, but . . . I don't know. There's something

172

about that mother-daughter bond. Something primal. I think we internalize more than we know."

For a second, I have the crazy urge to tell her about Stella. But inviting Eleni into my head would be insanity. I don't want to live in the same house with her, let alone make her think we're bonded for life.

"He still loves her, you know." I focus on my milk shake as I say it. "He still loves my mom. He *told* me."

"I know."

I look up.

She's smiling. "He told me, too. The day we met. Then again on the day we were married."

She seems to be great with this — which boggles my mind. "Why would anyone want to marry a man who still loves his wife?" I say. "Why would anyone do that to themselves?" I'm making her sound like an idiot, and part of me feels bad — but another part really wants to know.

She doesn't respond at first. While she swirls a french fry around in ketchup, I think about everything I'll say next. *My mom was the most positive person Birdie ever knew. Her smile could light up a room. She didn't just walk, she bounced.*

"Well," she says finally, "love is complicated."

Then she tells me about the day her mother died. It was cancer, she says, and it happened fast — only a few months after the diagnosis. They set up a bed in the living room, a real hospital bed, with a morphine drip attached.

She says that her father never left her mother's side, not once. He slept in the bed with her. He fed her ice chips. He refused to hire a nurse. "This is my wife," is what he said. "In sickness and in health." Eleni tears up a little when she says this and blows her nose on the burger wrapper.

She describes what her mother looked like in the end — the gray cast of her skin, the sunken eyes, the bald patches — but her father still said, "Good morning, beautiful," the way he always had. He still kissed her on the lips.

They were so in love, Eleni says, that she, an only child, sometimes felt excluded. On that day, she ran home to see her mother — she had a poem she'd written in English class, and she wanted to read it; her mom loved poetry — but her father wouldn't let her come in. He'd said they wanted some time alone — why didn't she go clean the bathroom and come back later? But there was no later. Her mother died while Eleni was scrubbing the bathtub.

"The single most defining moment of my life, and I missed it for something ordinary. This mundane task, scrubbing the tub." Her voice gets soft. "I never got to say good-bye."

I'm afraid she might cry again, but her face looks calm.

"Were you mad?" I ask. "At your dad?"

She nods. "For a long time. It took me years before I realized he wasn't being selfish; he was trying to protect me. I had to be a parent myself before I fully understood. Parents will do anything to protect their children."

She looks straight at me. "It's the most powerful form of love there is."

I wait for her to make her point, to tie everything together in a neat little bow, but she doesn't.

All she says is, "You'll understand one day. When you become a mom, you'll see."

She goes back to the fries, and that's when I realize I need to know more. I can't believe I want her to keep going, but I do.

"Did your dad get married again?" I ask.

She shakes her head. "He was never the same after that. He just . . . checked out. It was a very lonely time, for both of us. I think . . ." She pauses, swallows. "I *know* that's why I wanted to have a lot of kids. I never wanted to be that alone again."

"You couldn't be alone in your house if you tried," I say. "And believe me, I've tried."

She smiles. "It can be a challenge."

Then she asks if having my own room would make any difference. She could move her study into the den — or, if I'd be willing to wait until fall, when Thalia leaves for college, I could have the attic.

I can't believe she's offering this. I can't believe how nice she's being.

Please, I think. *Don't make me like you.*

"I stole money from your purse," I blurt out, "that night I took off. A *lot* of money. And I spent it."

She nods, as though she already knew. "I'm glad you told me," she says. "Thank you."

No matter what I say, no matter how much of a juvenile delinquent I am, she doesn't get mad.

I look at her. "If you want to ground me, you can. I don't have a job or anything, so I don't know how I'd pay you back, but —"

"I'm not worried about the money. You'll make it up to me."

"How?" I say.

She pats her belly. "Babysitting." Big smile. "Hours and hours of babysitting."

We're home. Eleni wedges her car into a parking spot, turns off the ignition, and unsnaps her seat belt.

Just as she's opening the door, the words fly out of my mouth. "I think I remember her smell."

She turns to me. Her eyes say, *Go on.*

So I try to describe it — the lemon-lavender-vanilla-wafer combo that is Stella. "It's like . . . here's what it is: walking into a flower store and a bakery at the same time."

"Mmm," she says. "That sounds nice."

"You don't think I'm crazy?"

"No." Her face is serious. "No, I don't."

I look at her and see that there are lines around her mouth, but they are nice lines — laugh lines. And her eyes are hazel like mine, which I never realized. I always thought they were plain brown. And there's a blob of ketchup in her hair.

This gives me the nerve to keep going. I tell her I used to talk to my mom sometimes, when I was younger. Not anymore, though.

Eleni raises her eyebrows as if to ask, *Why not?*

"I guess I grew up," I say.

She nods. Then, apparently, she changes her mind because now she's shaking her head.

"What?" I say.

"I don't know. I don't think you ever outgrow needing your parents."

In the silence that follows, I think of all the possible questions I could ask. What does she miss about her mom? What happened to her father? And how about her ex-husband — the one who didn't want to do the "parenting thing" and ran off with Tiffany the nineteen-year-old? Does she still love him? Did she keep the wedding photos or burn them?

Finally, I decide.

"Why my dad anyway?" I ask. "Why'd you marry Birdie?"

And what I'm thinking is, *Please don't tell me it's just because you were pregnant.*

She smiles, and I see that she's looking at the weirdo standing by the curb — in his overalls and safety goggles, waving a hammer. There's sawdust in his hair and a big green paint smudge on his cheek. He's chewing something and grinning maniacally at the same time. Any sane person would see him and think, *Okay, what nuthouse let him out?*

"Come on," Eleni says, laughing as Birdie pretends to hammer the windshield. "What's not to love?"

I think, *You got that right.*

But when she gets out of the car to kiss him, I make my eyes roll skyward. I make my mouth say, "Will you guys cool it? *God.*" The opposite of how I'm really feeling.

At dinner, I'm choking down a lamb kebab when Phoebe goes ballistic. "Eyelash!" she screams, practically poking me in the eye with her skewer. "Eyelasheyelasheyelash! Make a wish!"

"I don't make wishes," I say. "I don't believe in them."

She gives me a crushed look, like I just told her I stomp puppies for fun.

There's a barrette in her hair — a green plastic turtle — that reminds me of how young and clueless she is. Of course she still believes in wishes, and the tooth fairy, and world peace. She's still innocent. She hasn't figured out how messy and scary and sad life can be.

"Okay," I say. "Fine. Where is it?"

I let her wipe the eyelash off my cheek and transfer it from her pinky to mine.

"Close your eyes," she says. "You have to close your eyes."

Yeah, yeah, yeah. I don't need some pip-squeak telling me about wishing. I've been wishing twice as long as she's been alive. I'm a professional.

Close the eyes.

Breathe in.

And there it is. The only wish I have ever wished. The wish that's so familiar, it's like the security blanket Jules's sister, Agnes, has slept with for twenty years. It's a grayish, moth-eaten scrap that smells like eggs — but she took it with her to Yale anyway.

I picture myself at twenty, going to sleep in my dorm room with the same ratty old wish curled up next to me. It makes me sad to think about it.

So I try to think of a new one. I tell myself that the next wish that pops into my head will be it. And when I hear what it is, I'm surprised — shocked, really — but I decide to use it anyway.

Please let this baby be healthy. Thanks.

Then I open my eyes and blow that eyelash into oblivion.

In bed, with the sweater twins snoring away in the background, I try to picture the baby. Like one of those mismatch puzzles with the body parts, I pair Eleni's curly hair with Birdie's beak nose; his big ears with her cupid's bow mouth; her hips, his chicken legs. It's not pretty.

Then I picture a clear night like tonight, when I will wrap the kid up in a blanket — something yellow and fleecy, with ducks — and we'll go out into the backyard. The stars won't be anything great, not like Maine, but maybe we'll lie down on the ground anyway and look up. I'll hold its little dumpling hand and say, "Look, there's the Big Dipper. See? And the North Star." And it'll turn to me and smile with its gums, like an old fogy, and I'll say, "That's right. Polaris."

Probably something annoying will happen after that. Eleni will come out with some baklava, or one of the sweater twins will chuck the other one's curling iron out the window. But we will have had our moment anyway. Me and my baby sister. Or brother. Or whatever it is.

CHAPTER TWENTY-FOUR

Six A.M. and I'm already up. It's cold in the backyard. There's frost on the lawn chairs. I can see my breath.

I don't know why my brother came out here to sit with me, but he did. Probably because no one else is awake yet and he's bored.

"So," I say, "tonight's the night, huh?"

Mackey doesn't say anything. He just yanks up his collar over his ears and nods.

"Where's the dreamcoat, Joey? Shouldn't you be, you know, *getting into character* right about now?"

Grunt.

"Jules is coming. Her train gets in at three-fifty. Linus is picking her up. Can you believe she's *finally* coming to Boston? I mean, it's been —"

"I can't do it," he says, cutting me off.

I turn to face him. "What?"

"I can't get up in front of all those people and sing tonight."

"Well," I say, "you should have thought about that in September. It's a little late now."

But I can see how panicky he is. His eyes are all blinky, and his fingernails are bitten-down stumps, and I feel bad.

"Hey," I say. "Nerves are a good thing, right?"

Mackey doesn't answer. He stares at Clam's empty dog-house for a while. Chews on his nails. Stares. Chews.

Finally, he turns to me. "Want to know something crazy?"

"Yeah."

"When Birdie told us we were moving, I was happy."

I stare at him. "Ex*cuse* me?"

"I thought, okay, maybe I don't have to be the class dork anymore. Nobody knows me there. I could reinvent myself. Dress different. Act different. I could be anyone, you know? So when Thalia dragged me to that audition I thought, what the hell? Why not? So I tried out. I just didn't think I'd . . . I didn't expect to get the *part.*"

"Huh," I say.

It's not what Mackey's saying; it's the fact that he's talking to me at all that's mind-boggling. And he's not even done talking yet. He actually *keeps going.*

"Not that I'm not glad I got the part. I mean, I am. Do you know people talk to me at school now? Even the so-called popular kids? They call me Joseph."

I snort a little at this. I can't help it.

"I know," Mackey says. "But it's better than Pizza Face."

"True."

I squint at my brother, trying to see him through new eyes. His hair is brushed for once. And his face is almost clear — no more pepperoni nose.

"Hey," I say. "Your skin looks better. I'm not just saying that, it really does."

"Yeah. Clio gave me some kind of cream."

"Really? *Clio?*"

"Yeah."

He goes on to tell me how he finally has a table to sit at for lunch, with the theater crowd. Thalia sits there, too. And this guy Pete. And this girl Sandra, who's gorgeous. There's a whole bunch of them. Finally, it seems, he's beginning to fit in.

"So . . ." I say. "Most people would call that a *good* thing."

"Right," he says.

"So?"

"It's so good I don't want to screw it up. I can't afford to screw it up. But what if I do? What if tonight, I suck?"

I can see how freaked out he is, and I want him to believe me when I say, "You won't suck. You'll be great."

"Mmf."

"What is it people in showbiz say? *Break a leg?* Well, that seems like bad karma to me. *Break a leg.* I'm not going to tell you to twist an ankle and fall down on the stage, writhing in pain. That's just wrong."

"It's supposed to be ironic," Mackey says. "Reverse psychology. For luck."

"I don't care what it is. I'm not saying it. And me *not* saying it will bring you luck. *Reverse* reverse psychology."

"You're weird, you know that?"

"You think *I'm* weird," I say, "you should see what the freak shows in there are wearing tonight." I flip a thumb toward the house.

"What? The GLUE shirts?"

"Oh, no. Worse."

"What?"

"You'll see," I say. "After your spectacular, awe-inspiring, Tony-caliber performance tonight, you'll see what those people are wearing. And you'll run screaming in the other direction."

"Ah." Mackey nods. "*Those people.*"

I remind him that I don't enjoy participating in any rah-rah family-bonding activities. "All we do around here lately is act like idiots," I say. I cite the most recent offense: Birdie's birthday, when we all went out to dinner at Spaghetti Freddie's wearing "I Love Al" buttons that lit up and played the Macarena.

"It's humiliating, Mack. It's *mortifying* being with them in public."

"Come on," he says. "You had fun. Admit it."

"No. I *hate* the Macarena. I only danced for Birdie."

"Uh-huh," he says. "So, will you be wearing tonight's mystery outfit?"

"Please. Like I have a choice. Like anyone has a choice in this family."

My brother smiles. He hardly ever smiles. It's weird.

"What?" I say.

"You do realize you just called them your family."

"*What?* No, I didn't."

"Yeah. You did."

I shrug. "So?"

"So?" He says this in a teasey voice, the way brothers are supposed to, to drive their sisters crazy.

"Okay, fine," I say. "It *was* nice of them to have that party for Birdie. I had an okay time. Whatever."

Mackey says, "Whatever."

He is still grinning, and I am deciding whether I want to hit him right now. I decide not to, but only because tonight is his big night and I feel bad for him.

"You can shut up now," I say. "And I'll make you oatmeal."

The auditorium is packed. It's opening night, a sold-out show, and I'm so nervous for Mackey I can hardly breathe. Thankfully, Jules is here to distract me.

"Your brothers are so *hot*. I can't believe you never told me how hot your brothers are." She doesn't even bother keeping her voice down.

"Stepbrothers," I whisper. "Please."

"Still," she says. "Hubba hubba."

I consider telling her about my Linus crush, then think better of it. That is yesterday's news. So, apparently, is Pamela, because tonight he showed up with a new girl, Clementine.

"Like the fruit?" Phoebe asked at dinner.

"Like the folk song," Linus said.

Of course Birdie couldn't contain himself. He had to bust out "Oh, my darlin'" at the top of his whistle. He kept it up all through dinner, until Clio finally lost it. "Al! You're driving us nuts!"

"Okay," he said, and stopped. But now he's at it again. I can hear him, four seats over, whistling away.

"I can't believe your dad," Jules says. "He looks completely different. He's so . . . *dapper*."

"I know," I say.

I look at Birdie, in his white oxford shirt and khakis and mustache. The mustache is new. It's supposed to be a compromise between the beard and nothing, but nobody likes it. Well, Phoebe does, but she's the only one. Right now, she's on his lap. Normally, she would be sitting on Eleni, but there's no room anymore. This baby is going to be a bruiser. Already, we are placing bets. My guess is fifteen pounds, three ounces. If I win, it's no diaper duty for the first month.

"I can't believe any of it," Jules says. "You have, like, this whole new family. It's so weird."

"I know."

I look at everyone. The GLUE Crew. We take up an entire row.

I look at Thalia and Cleanser Boy and Linus and Eleni and Birdie and Phoebe and the sweater twins — who I can finally tell apart; it's all about the tiny mole on Cassi's left cheek. The "carcinoma-waiting-to-happen," as Clio calls it. ("Shut up, Clio! It's a beauty mark!")

When Ajax catches my eye, he grins and rolls his fingers around each other in a circle.

I make a throttling gesture back at him.

"What's that supposed to mean?" Jules says. "What are you doing? Sign language?"

"Nothing," I say. "It's stupid."

So stupid. Ajax came to my room a few nights ago and said he knew something I didn't know. He knew someone who liked me — someone who thought I was "sassy."

Jules snorts. "*Sassy?*"

"Yeah. And when I asked him who, he gave me a hint. Toilet paper."

"That was his sign for *toilet paper?*"

"I told you it was stupid."

"So," she says. "Who is it?"

"No one. He's messing with me. It's probably some bra-stuffing joke. Eighth-grade boys are so mature."

"Come on. You don't know anyone with the initials *T.P.?*"

I look at her. "What?"

"Toilet paper. *T.P.*"

Oh my God.

"No way," I say, shaking my head.

Travis Piesch likes me.

"What?" Jules says.

"Nothing." *Travis Piesch likes me.* "Just this kid in my Latin class."

"Johnny Depp's dork-twin?"

"Uh-huh."

"So. Do you like him?"

"He's not my type," I say.

"Fine," she says. "So. Do you like him?"

"*Jules.*"

"Just answer the question."

"Um. I don't know yet."

She laughs. "Your face is so red right now."

"That's because it's hot in here! Come on! I'm about to die from the heat!"

"I know," she says. "I'm sweltering. How long do we have to wear these things, anyway?"

She yanks at the scarf around her neck — the fluorescent-patchwork-quilt pattern with the fringe hanging off it. Thalia made it. She made them all.

"Don't even *think* about removing the Dream Scarf," I say. "We're showing our solidarity. For Joseph."

Jules gives me a look.

"I know," I say. "I know."

It's weird. It's weird how you can go from hating something with a passion to thinking that it may not be entirely horrible after all.

It's not that I don't still miss Maine. I do. I miss my old room, with the real backyard, and the ocean down the street. I miss it being just the three Linneys sometimes, eating chicken from a bucket.

It's not that Eleni suddenly stopped bugging me, or that the sweater twins stopped fighting, or that I'm entirely thrilled about this love child coming, or that ever since I started wearing Stella's necklace again, I've been remembering to bounce more often. It's just . . . I don't know what it is.

Maybe I'm just happy Jules came. Later, I'll take her by C.B.'s to meet the girls. We'll stay up all night, dancing around like maniacs and eating Fritos with Cheez Whiz.

But right now, the lights are going down.

The lights are going down, and everyone's getting quiet.

Darkness is seeping in all around.

I can feel my palms, damp against my knees. I can feel my heart, bumping against my throat.

Tonight is so big.

Stella?

I close my eyes. I can't help it. I picture a balcony seat, one with a spectacular view. Maybe some of those old-fashioned opera glasses.

Stell?

And even though I can't see her anymore, even though I can barely conjure her smell, I can feel her. Somehow, crazy as it sounds, I know she's here.

Thank you, I whisper.

"Holy crap." Jules leans in and grabs my leg. "I can't believe I'm in *Boston*! I can't believe I'm actually —"

"Shhhh," I say.

Because now the orchestra is revving up. The curtains are opening. My brother — my sci-fi-reading, Birkenstock-wearing, dragon-slaying, computer-geek brother — is about to take the stage.

And I don't want to miss it.